She touched the hair curling at the nape of his neck, wanting the kiss to never stop.

At the sound of Max ringing the chow bell, he let her go. She drew back, shaken by the kiss. "We shouldn't have done that."

"I'm not going to apologize for kissing you. I've wanted to since the first time I laid eyes on you. Only back then, I was just a boy who thought the way to get a girl's attention was to give her a hard time."

"I'm still a married woman," she said, hating that she sounded breathless. Had she ever been kissed like that? "And I'm your boss."

He nodded. "If you're saying that I have bad timing, I couldn't agree more." He grinned. "But I'm still not sorry." With that, he touched her cheek, a light caress, before he rose, retrieved his shirt from the tree, pulled on his boots and left, saying, "I'll see you back in camp, boss."

AMBUSH BEFORE SUNRISE

New York Times Bestselling Author
B.J. DANIELS

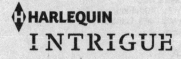

HARLEQUIN
INTRIGUE

This book is for anyone who's fallen for the wrong person—and
gotten lucky and found the right one. It's never too late for love.

HARLEQUIN
INTRIGUE

Recycling programs
for this product may
not exist in your area.

ISBN-13: 978-1-335-13579-7

Ambush before Sunrise

Copyright © 2020 by Barbara Heinlein

This edition published by arrangement with Harlequin Books S.A.

For questions and comments about the quality of this book,
please contact us at CustomerService@Harlequin.com.

Harlequin Enterprises ULC
22 Adelaide St. West, 40th Floor
Toronto, Ontario M5H 4E3, Canada
www.Harlequin.com

Printed in U.S.A.

B.J. Daniels is a *New York Times* and *USA TODAY* bestselling author. She wrote her first book after a career as an award-winning newspaper journalist and author of thirty-seven published short stories. She lives in Montana with her husband, Parker, and three springer spaniels. When not writing, she quilts, boats and plays tennis. Contact her at bjdaniels.com, on Facebook or on Twitter, @bjdanielsauthor.

Books by B.J. Daniels

Harlequin Intrigue

Cardwell Ranch: Montana Legacy

Steel Resolve
Iron Will
Ambush before Sunrise

Whitehorse, Montana: The Clementine Sisters

Hard Rustler
Rogue Gunslinger
Rugged Defender

The Montana Cahills

Cowboy's Redemption

Whitehorse, Montana: The McGraw Kidnapping

Dark Horse
Dead Ringer
Rough Rider

HQN Books

Montana Justice

Restless Hearts
Heartbreaker

Sterling's Montana

Stroke of Luck
Luck of the Draw
Just His Luck

The Montana Cahills

Renegade's Pride
Outlaw's Honor
Hero's Return
Rancher's Dream

Visit the Author Profile page at Harlequin.com.

CAST OF CHARACTERS

JoRay "Jinx" McCallahan—She married the wrong man and now he's trying to destroy her. Her only hope of saving her ranch is three wranglers from Cardwell Ranch.

Angus Cardwell Savage—When he heard Jinx needed help, he saddled up. The cowboy had never forgotten the redheaded girl. He can't wait to see the woman she's become.

Brick Cardwell Savage—From the beginning, he had a bad feeling about going to Wyoming to help Jinx.

Ella Cardwell—She can rope and ride as well as her male cousins. But even she can see that this is going to be their last rodeo.

TD Sharp—When he married Jinx, he thought he'd won the lottery. Now she thought she could divorce him? He'd rather see her dead.

Wyatt Hanson—He'd been TD's best friend since they were boys in spite of the way the cowboy treated him. But now he wants something of TD's and sees a way to get it.

Patty Conroe—TD's mistress wants Jinx gone and is willing to sell her soul to make it happen.

Harvey Bessler—Jinx is like a daughter to the sheriff. But not even he can protect her from the man she married.

Chapter One

JoRay "Jinx" McCallahan stormed into the sheriff's office, mad, frustrated and just plain beside herself.

Sheriff Harvey Bessler looked up from his desk in surprise, saw her and groaned good-naturedly. "Let me guess. T.D.?"

"What am I supposed to do about him? I'm already divorcing him. I've got a restraining order against him—like that does a lick of good. I've run him off with a shotgun. But short of shooting him, he just keeps coming back."

"All you have to do is call when he breaks the restraining order on him and we'll pick him up."

"And he'll be back on the street within hours even madder and more determined to drive me crazy."

Harvey nodded sympathetically. "Unfortunately, we don't have anything else we can hold him on. Unless he is caught in the act doing something illegal…" The sheriff motioned her into a chair before he leaned back in his own to eye her over the top of his cheater glasses. "How are you doing other than that?"

She scoffed as she took a seat. She'd been coming to this office since she was a child. Her father and Harvey had been best friends up until Ray McCallahan's recent death. Because of that, Harvey was like a second father to her. She'd been fortunate to have such good men in her life.

Until T. D. Sharp.

The sheriff got to his feet and came around his desk to call out to the receptionist. "Mabel, get this girl a cola from the machine. Get me one, too." He turned back to Jinx. "Remember when you were little and you'd come in here with your papa to visit? I'd always get you a cola. It always made you feel better."

Just the mention of her father made her eyes burn with tears. She missed him so much and she knew Harvey did, as well. "That was back when the worst thing that happened to me was falling off my bike and skinning my knees."

He laughed. "True enough. Not that you let a little thing like a skinned knee stop you. You've always been strong, Jinx."

She didn't feel strong as she heard Mabel come to the door with two bottles from the old-timey machine in the break room. Harvey took them and gently closed the door.

"I'm afraid this is the best I can do right now," he said as he handed over her cola. "What's T.D. done now?"

She took the drink, feeling embarrassed for the way she'd barged in here. T.D. wasn't Harvey's problem; he was hers. She took a sip from the bottle Mabel had opened for her. It was ice-cold. For a moment she felt like a kid again as the sheriff went around behind his desk and lowered his weight into his chair with a creak and groan.

"Other than bad-mouthing me all over town? He's got it where I can't find anyone to work out at the ranch and I've got cattle that if I don't get them to summer pasture…" Her voice broke. She took another sip.

"I don't doubt T.D. did everything you're saying," Harvey said quietly. "He been out to your place again?"

She waved that off, knowing if Harvey picked him up it would only make T.D. worse, if that were possible. She hadn't come here for that. She knew she had just needed to see him because she needed to vent and she knew that he'd listen. "I keep getting offers on the ranch even though it isn't for sale. T.D. is determined to take half of whatever I could get for the place, even though we were married such a short time. He actually thinks he deserves half the ranch."

Harvey shook his large gray head. "I'm sure you had your reasons for marrying him."

Jinx laughed. "You know that you and Dad tried to warn me but I was in...*love*." She practically spat the word out. "How could I have been so blind?"

"It happens, especially when it comes to love. T.D. can be quite charming, I've heard."

"Not for long." She took another long drink of her cola. "What does that leave me?" she asked, her voice sounding small and scared even to her. "I'm going to have to sell the ranch to get rid of him. My only other option is to—"

"You're not going to shoot him."

She smiled. "You sure about that?"

Harvey sighed. "I know things have been rough since Ray died. Maybe you should think about getting away for a while. Maybe take a trip somewhere. Give T.D. time to cool down."

She narrowed her eyes at him. "Or maybe I should sell the cattle and take a loss and forget about driving them up into the mountains to summer range." But that would be admitting defeat and she wasn't good at that. When backed against a wall, her tendency was to come out fighting, not give up.

He said nothing for a moment. "What did your father want you to do?" he asked quietly.

Jinx felt the shock move through her and realized of course her father had told his best friend what he wanted her to do once he was gone. "I'm going to have to sell the ranch, aren't I?"

"Sweetie, I know it's not what you want. Are you that determined to keep ranching?"

"It's all I know, but it's more than that. That place has been my home since I was born. I don't want to give it up just because of T.D."

"That's the real thorn in your side, isn't it? T.D. has you against the ropes. But I can't believe you're not that set on ranching it alone. Then again, you're so much like your father," Harvey said, smiling across the desk at her. "Stubborn as the day is long and just as proud. But if you're keeping the ranch to show T.D. or people in this town…"

"It isn't right that T.D. should force me into this or worse, take half."

"I agree. You hired yourself a good lawyer, right?"

She nodded. "He says T.D. can ask for half of what the ranch is worth on paper. No way can I come up with that kind of money. I don't have a choice. In the meantime, T.D. has it where I can't even find any wranglers to work for me."

His expression softened. "I'm worried about you. If T.D. breaks the restraining order again, you call me. I can pick him up, maybe even keep him overnight."

She shook her head, finished her cola and stood. "Thanks."

"I didn't do anything."

Jinx smiled at the older man. "You listened and the cola tasted just like it did when I was a kid. I do feel better. Thanks."

The sheriff rose, as well. As she started to take the empty bottle back to the break room, he said, "I'll take that." She handed it to him, their gazes meeting.

"I'm going to go have a talk with T.D.," he said and rushed on before she could say it would be a waste of time. "He's a cocky son of a bitch and I would love nothing better than to throw him behind bars—that's just between you and me. Maybe we'll get lucky and he'll take a swing at me."

She laughed. "Good luck with that. In the meantime, somehow I'm going to get my cattle to summer range. I'm not going to let T.D. stop me even if it means taking the cattle up there by myself. Don't worry, I've advertised out of state. Maybe I'll get lucky. After that…" She shook her head. She had no idea.

Her hope was that T.D. would give up. Or his girlfriend would keep him busy and away from her. Her father used to believe time healed most things. But with a man like T. D. Sharp? She had her doubts.

"Jinx?" She turned at the door to look back at the sheriff. "Just be careful, okay?"

T. D. SHARP THREW his legs over the side of the bed and hung his head. A cool breeze dried the sweat on his naked body as he sat for a moment fighting his mounting regrets and frustration. At the feel of a warm hand on his bare back, he fought the urge to shake it off.

"Come on, baby," Patty Conroe purred. "You don't have to leave. You just got here."

He reached for his underwear and jeans, anxious to escape. Coming here tonight had been a mistake. After his run-in with the sheriff earlier, he'd thought what he needed was a kind word and a soft, willing body. But it hadn't worked tonight. His body had performed but his mind had been miles away—out on the Flying J Bar MC Ranch.

"I need to go out to the ranch and talk to my wife," he said as he stood to pull on his jeans, foolishly voicing the thought that had been rattling around in his head. The sheriff thought he could threaten him? That old fool didn't know who he was dealing with. If T.D. needed to go talk to Jinx, he damned sure would. She could take her restraining order and stuff it up her—

"She isn't your *wife*," Patty snapped. "She's your *ex*."

"Not yet." He heard her sit up behind him. "We

don't sign the papers until the property settlement is finished and it sure ain't finished. Which means she's still my wife. And I can damn well go see her if I want to."

"What about the restraining order? You go near her and she's going to call the sheriff."

"Let her. She already went whining to him, but there isn't a thing he can do to me. Anyway, I'm not afraid of Harvey Bessler."

"He's the law, T.D. You better watch yourself or he'll trump something up and lock you behind bars. Have you forgotten that he was her father's best friend? He would love nothing better than to put you in one of his cells."

He scoffed, more than aware how tight Ray McCallahan had been with the sheriff. But Ray was dead and gone and if Harvey kept harassing him, he'd get the old fart fired. "Let him try."

"You think he won't arrest you? Well, I'm not getting you out of jail this time. You hear me? *Let Jinx go.* She sure didn't have any trouble letting *you* go."

Her words were like a gut punch. He wanted to slap her mouth. "Watch it," he warned. He wouldn't put up with her saying anything bad about Jinx, whether the woman was his almost-ex-wife or not.

He looked around for his boots, knowing that if he didn't get out of this apartment and soon, they were going to fight. He was already fighting with Jinx. He didn't need another woman on his case.

"Why do you need to talk to her *tonight*? Anyway, shouldn't your lawyer be handling this?"

He didn't answer, knowing better. He wished he hadn't brought the subject up about his soon-to-be ex to start with. But she'd been on his mind. Nothing new there. Jinx had caught his eye and he'd fallen for the woman. Fallen hard. When she'd told him it was over and sent him packing, he'd been in shock. The woman needed him. How was she going to run that ranch without him?

But somehow she'd managed in the months since he'd been booted out. He'd put the word out that no one he knew had better go to work for her if they knew what was good for them. He chuckled to himself since he'd heard she was having trouble hiring wranglers to take her cattle up to summer range.

That would teach her to kick him to the curb. He'd thought for sure that after a week or two she'd realize the mistake she'd made and beg him to come back. So he'd made a few mistakes. Like hooking up with Patty.

But Patty wasn't even the reason that Jinx had thrown him out. She'd said she didn't care about his girlfriend, his drinking, his not working the ranch like he should have. She said she was just over him and wanted him gone.

Maybe as his friends said, the only reason he wanted her back was because of his bruised and battered ego. But he knew in his heart that wasn't all of it. He still wanted Jinx. She was the sexiest woman he knew. He was crazy about her.

If she hadn't made him feel like he was a hired hand, he wouldn't have needed Patty. But from the day they married, he'd been too aware that it was her ranch. Not that she didn't always tell him that it was their ranch and that was why she wanted him more involved. But he knew better.

Once she threw him out, though, he threw her words back at her. *Our ranch, huh? Well, then I want half of it.* Not that it was even about the ranch and the property settlement anymore. He couldn't stand that he'd let a woman like her get away. Just the thought of another man touching her drove him insane.

He told himself he could change. He could be the man she needed. She had to give him another chance. He figured if the two of them could just talk—or even better, hit the sack together—they could work this out. Once he got her in bed, she'd listen to reason.

"You're bound and determined to go out there, aren't you?" Patty said behind him, sounding close to tears. She was wasting her time. Her tears no longer moved him. For months she'd been trying to get him to divorce Jinx and marry her. The woman was delusional.

"Maybe I should drive out to that ranch myself," she said, sniffing dramatically. He heard the threat, the anger, the spite, dripping with jealousy. "I'd like to tell her what I think of her."

T.D. refused to take the bait as he found his boots and began to tug them on. Now, if he could just find his shirt…

"I think it would do her good to know that you've been sneaking over to my place the whole time you've been married to her. Her lawyer might want to hear about it, too."

The words swung at him like a baseball bat to the back of his head. He spun around, going for her throat before he could call back his fury. The woman was threatening to ruin *everything*. Before she could move he was on her. He saw the shock and fear in her eyes as his large hands clamped around her scrawny neck. She opened her mouth, gasping like a fish tossed up on the bank, but no sound came out.

He'd known about the bad blood between Jinx and Patty. Apparently, they'd gone to school together. Jinx had dated Patty's brother in high school. When the fool had gotten drunk and driven off the switchbacks on the highway west of Jackson Hole, Patty was convinced that he'd done it on purpose because of his breakup with Jinx.

T.D. had known how jealous Patty was of Jinx. He'd always suspected that was the reason she'd come after him, determined to get him into her bed not long after his marriage to Jinx. As if it took a lot of effort on her part. Patty was a nice-enough-looking woman with willing ways.

But tonight she seemed to have forgotten her place in the scheme of things. Leaning closer, he tightened his hold on her throat and, pressing his lips to her ear, whispered, "You listen to me. You won't go near that ranch. You won't go near Jinx. You ever say a word to her and I'll..." He felt her go limp and let go of her, dropping her back on the pillows.

For a moment he thought he'd killed her, but then she came to, gasping, eyes wild, hands going to her red and bruising throat. He watched her wheeze for breath as she scooted across the bed out of his reach.

Good, he thought. She needed to know exactly what she was dealing with if she ever betrayed him. She'd been getting a little too cocky for her own good lately. All that talk about the two of them getting married as soon as his divorce went through. Like he would tie a noose around his neck again, especially with a woman like her.

He found his shirt and pulled it on. As he walked out, he didn't look back. Let her wonder if he would ever return. Women like Patty Conroe were a dime a dozen. Women like JoRay "Jinx" McCallahan were another story.

Regret flooded him as he climbed behind the wheel of his pickup. He'd blown it with Jinx. Talk about cocky. Once he had that ring on her finger, he thought he could just coast with her. He'd been dead wrong.

Letting out a snort, he still couldn't believe that she was going to divorce him, though. But then again when Jinx threatened to do something, look out, because the woman was going to do it, come hell or high water.

As he started the engine, he reached over and pulled a can of beer from the near-empty six-pack he'd left on the seat. He told himself that he'd get Jinx back because he couldn't live without her. He knew that now, he thought as he opened the beer and took a long pull on it.

Admittedly, he shouldn't have cheated on her. He should have helped out around the ranch more. He should have done a lot of things differently. With a second chance, he would.

Not that it was all his fault. Jinx wasn't an easy woman. She was too damned independent. Truth was, she didn't need him and that stuck in his craw.

But now with her daddy in his grave, Jinx was all alone except for Max, that old cook of hers—

and all those cattle that needed to be taken up to summer range in the high country.

Maybe she would realize that she couldn't live without him, either. He'd heard that she was so desperate she had even advertised for wranglers out of state.

T.D. smiled to himself. Thanks to him, she was high and dry right now. No one around here was going to work for her. He knew most of the wranglers for hire because of all the years he'd gone from ranch to ranch as one. Unless they wanted to get on his wrong side—a bad place to be—they'd stay clear of Jinx and her ranch. And they had.

What better time to have a talk with her, he thought feeling good. He'd make sure it was just the two of them, restraining order or not. He'd charmed her into marrying him. Surely, he could charm his way back into her life—and her bed.

JINX MCCALLAHAN SLOWED her pickup as she spotted two trucks and horse trailers sitting in her ranch yard. She didn't recognize either of them. After parking, she climbed out and took in the group waiting for her.

She shoved back her Western hat as she considered what looked like a straggly bunch of wranglers standing in the glow of her yard light. She told herself that beggars couldn't be choosers since she had several hundred head of Herefords to get into the high country and time was running out.

Normally, she had no trouble hiring on help this time of year. She was no fool. Her inability to find local help was T.D.'s doing. He'd put the word out, forcing her to look for help much farther from home, but hadn't heard anything. Unfortunately, word traveled fast among ranching communities about her "problems" with her soon-to-be ex-husband. She couldn't blame anyone for not wanting to get into the middle of it, especially if they knew anything about T. D. Sharp.

But after stopping at the sheriff's office, she'd run some errands, bought herself some dinner and made up her mind. She wasn't going to let T.D. put her out of business even if she had to take the herd to summer range all by herself—just as she'd told the sheriff. Maybe she wouldn't have to if any of these wranglers were decent hands, she thought now.

She stepped to the first cowboy who'd climbed out of the trucks and stood waiting for her. As he removed his hat, she looked into the bluest eyes she'd ever seen and felt a start. Was it the scar on his chin or something about his eyes? What was it about him that made her think she knew this man? Or had at least run across him sometime before? Surely, she would have remembered if she had stumbled across such a handsome cowboy.

Stress and lack of sleep, she told herself. Her mind was playing tricks on her. Or her body was. Because she felt strangely close to him as if they'd once shared something almost…intimate? She knew that was crazy. There'd never been that many men in her life.

Jinx shook her head. Her father's illness, his death, T.D.… All of it had taken a toll on her, she knew. She couldn't trust her mind or her body or her instincts. And if she and this man had met, wouldn't he have said something?

"What's your name?" she asked him.

"Angus Cardwell Savage, ma'am."

"Cardwell?" Her eyes narrowed. "Any relation to the Cardwell Ranch in Montana?"

"Dana Cardwell Savage is my mother."

She considered the tall, lanky, good-looking cowboy for a moment, telling herself that she had to be wrong about having met him before and stepped to the next one. "And you're…"

He quickly removed his hat. "Brick Cardwell Savage, ma'am."

She felt a start as she did a double take, looking from Angus to Brick and back. "You're twins?"

"Identical," Brick said with a chuckle. "Except I'm more charming."

Jinx ignored that. A charming cowboy was the last thing she needed. She'd married one and look how that had turned out.

She considered the two for a moment. Angus had a small scar on his chin in the shape of a crescent moon. Other than that, she couldn't tell the brothers apart. She moved on to the next wrangler.

As the cowhand removed the weathered straw hat, a long blond braid tumbled out. "Ella Cardwell," the wrangler said, lifting her chin in obvious defiance.

Jinx shook her head. "I said I needed men. Not—"

"I can do anything these two can do," Ella said, aiming her elbow at the two cowboys next to her who were also from Cardwell Ranch. "Usually better," the cowgirl added, lifting her gaze until Jinx was staring into emerald green eyes that flashed with fire.

She shot a glance at the two Cardwell men, expecting them to object. Neither did. Turning back to the young woman, she said, "Ella Cardwell, huh?"

"My mother's Stacy Cardwell. Dana's my aunt."

"What are you doing riding with these two?" Jinx asked, indicating Ella's cousins.

"I like wrangling. I'm more at home on the back of a horse than anywhere on this earth." She shrugged. "My cousins watch out for me and I watch out for them."

Jinx studied the young woman whom she estimated to be in her late twenties, early thirties—about her own age and that of her cousins. They were all young when what she needed was seasoned help. Unfortunately, there was none to be had right now because of her almost-ex-husband. It was why she couldn't afford to be picky and yet…

"Why aren't you all working on your family ranch?" she asked, concerned about their ages and lack of experience. Also their possible safety, given what was going on.

"I will someday, but in the meantime, we wanted to see more of the country and experience life before we settled down," Angus said.

Brick chuckled. "Just sowing some wild oats, ma'am."

That was what she was afraid of. "There won't be any of that on this cattle drive. We have to get my herd up into the mountains for the summer and I'm already running late. If you're looking for fun, you've come to the wrong place."

"We're good hands and we aren't afraid of hard work, ma'am," Angus said, giving his brother's boot next to him a kick. "Don't mind my brother. He likes to joke, ma'am."

She'd had more than enough of this ma'am stuff. "Call me Jinx," she said as she moved to the next two wranglers who'd answered her help-wanted ad.

"Royce Richards," said the fourth cowboy. At

least he was older. "Cash and me here used to wrangle for—"

"Huck Chambers," Jinx said, nodding as she eyed the men more closely. She'd seen them around Jackson Hole. Cash looked to be in his early forties, much like Royce. He removed his hat and said, "Cash Andrews." While Royce was tall and wiry-thin with a narrow, pinched face and deep-set dark eyes, Cash was larger with a broad face as plain as a prairie. But when her eyes met his pale brown ones she felt something unsettling behind them.

She tried to remember what she'd heard about the men and why they were no longer with Huck. She thought about calling Huck, but told herself if they didn't work out, she'd pay them off and send them packing. She only needed them for a few days, a week at most, depending on the weather and how long it would take them to move the cattle.

Looking the lot of them over, she reminded herself that she was desperate, but was she *this* desperate? She hesitated. She could use all of them, but hiring a young woman wrangler? That seemed like a recipe for disaster on a cattle drive. She thought of the spirit she'd seen in the young woman's eyes, a spirit that reminded her of herself.

"All right," she said with a sigh, hoping she wasn't making a mistake—not just with the

Cardwell bunch but with Royce and maybe especially Cash. What was that she'd seen in his gaze? Just a flicker of something she couldn't put her finger on. A lot of cowboys didn't like taking orders from a woman. She hoped that was all she'd seen.

"See your way to the bunkhouse. We ride out at first light in the morning. I notice that you brought your own stock," she said, glancing at the two pickups parked in her yard and the horse trailers behind them. "You can bed them down for the night in the barn or that corral. Cook will rustle up something for you to eat. I wouldn't suggest going into Jackson Hole tonight." *Or any other night*, she thought. But since they would ride into the mountains early tomorrow, they'd have little chance to get into trouble.

At least that was what she told herself as she headed inside the ranch house to talk to Max about feeding them. She found him in the kitchen finishing up washing some pots and pans, his back to her. The cook was short and stocky as a fat thumb with a personality as surprising as what he often cooked. He'd been with Jinx's family for years. She didn't know what she would do without him. Or vice versa if she sold the ranch.

But as she studied the man from behind, she realized Max was getting old. He wouldn't be able to handle a cattle drive much longer. For him, her selling the ranch might be a relief. He could retire since she knew her father had left him well-off.

The moment he turned around and she saw Max's face, she knew he'd seen her wranglers. "They might not be as bad as they look," she said defensively.

"Didn't say a word."

"You didn't have to." She leaned on the counter. "Can you rustle up something for them to eat?"

He nodded and began digging in the refrigerator. He came out with a chunk of roast beef. She watched him slice it and said, "They're young, I'll admit."

"Unless my eyes are going, that one looked distinctly female."

She sighed. "I like her."

Max laughed, shaking his head. "Bet she reminds you of yourself."

"Is that so bad?" He said nothing, letting that be his answer. "You hear anything about Royce Richards and Cash Andrews?" she asked, changing the subject. "They used to work for Huck Chambers."

He looked up from the beef he was slicing. "If you have any misgivings, send them on down the road."

"I can't. I have to take a chance with them. I need the help and at least they're older and probably more experienced." She looked toward the window and wondered what her father would have done. In the twilight, the pine trees were etched black against the graying sky. Beyond that, the dark outline of the mountains beckoned.

She told herself that she had to follow her instincts. First, she would get the herd up to the high country to graze for the summer. It would buy her time. Then she would decide what to do. She couldn't think about the future right now.

But of course that was all that was on her mind. "Once this cattle drive is over…" She didn't finish because she didn't know what she would do. Just the thought of ever leaving this ranch brought her to tears.

"I'll run sandwiches over to the bunkhouse," Max said. "You should get some sleep. You worry too much. You have five wranglers. With a little luck—"

"My luck's been running pretty thin lately." If the wranglers had heard what was going on at her ranch, they wouldn't have wanted anything to do with the Flying J Bar MC and she'd really be out of luck.

"I have a feeling your luck is about to change for the better," Max said as he picked up the plate of sandwiches and started for the door. "You're due. You want one of these sandwiches? I don't remember you eating much for dinner earlier."

She shook her head. "I'm not hungry, but thanks. Max," she called, stopping him at the door. "You didn't have anything to do with those three showing up from Cardwell Ranch, right? You didn't call Dana Savage, did you?"

He didn't turn as he said, "Go behind your back? I know better than to do something like that. I'm no fool." With that he left.

Jinx sighed, still suspicious. Her mother had been friends with Dana and it would be just like Max to try to help any way he could. She let it go, telling herself not to look a gift horse in the mouth. She had five wranglers, and tomorrow they would head up into the high country. Maybe Max was right and her luck was changing.

Still, she stood for a long time in the kitchen, remembering how things had been when both of her parents were alive. This house had been filled with laughter. But it had been a long time ago, she thought as she heard Max leave the bunkhouse and head out to his cabin. Her father's recent illness and death had left a pall over the ranch even before she'd finally had it with T.D.

You need a change. Don't stay here and try to run this ranch by yourself. I don't want that for you. Her father's words still haunted her. Did he really think it would be that easy just to sell this place, something he and his father had built with their blood, sweat and tears?

She shook her head and was about to head up to bed when she heard the roar of a vehicle engine. Through the kitchen window, she spotted headlights headed her way—and coming fast. "T.D." She said his name like a curse.

Chapter Two

After they took care of their horses, Angus could tell that something was bothering his cousin and wasn't surprised when Ella pulled the two of them aside.

"Maybe we should have told her the truth about why we're here," she said, keeping her voice down. The other two wranglers were still inside the bunkhouse.

"I thought the plan wasn't to say anything unless she didn't hire us," Brick reminded her. "She hired us, so what's the problem?"

"It doesn't feel right keeping the truth from her," Ella said more to Angus than Brick. She knew how Brick felt. He'd found them a job up by the Canadian border where one of his old girlfriends lived on the ranch. The last thing he'd wanted to do was come to Wyoming instead. Especially knowing the circumstances.

"We don't want to stomp on the woman's pride," Angus said. He knew firsthand where that could get a person. "Jinx needs three good wranglers and that's what we're doing here. Once it's done you can go anywhere you want to go."

Brick sighed as they reached their pickup and unloaded their gear before continuing on to the bunkhouse. Angus found himself looking out into the growing darkness. He'd felt it the moment they'd driven into the ranch yard. He wondered if the others had, as well, but wasn't about to ask. Trouble had a feel to it that hung in the air. An anticipation. A dread. A sense of growing danger. It was thick as the scent of pines on this ranch.

He understood why his brother hadn't wanted to come—and not just because of that cowgirl up by the Canadian border. "Don't see any reason to buy trouble," Brick had argued. "I know this woman's mother was a good friend of our mother's, but *Wyoming*?" Brick had never seen any reason to leave Montana. Angus felt much the same way.

But Jinx McCallahan was in trouble and their mother had asked them to help her—but to keep in mind that she was a strong, independent woman who wouldn't take well to charity. She just needed some wranglers to get her cattle up to summer range, Dana had said.

While Brick had been dragging his feet, none of them was apt to turn down Dana Cardwell Savage. But what his brother and cousin didn't know was that he would have come even if their mother hadn't asked them. The moment he heard that JoRay "Jinx" McCallahan needed wranglers, he'd been on board.

"Once she can get her cattle up to summer range, things should get better for her," their mother had said. News among ranch families traveled like wildfire, but Angus had the feeling Dana had heard from someone close to Jinx. "The trouble is her ex-husband. He's got all the local ranchers riled up. She can't get anyone to work for her other than Max, the ranch cook, and while he's like family, he's getting up in age."

Angus had talked Brick into it. All it had taken was the promise that when the cattle were in their summer grazing area, they'd hightail it back to Montana.

Ella hadn't needed any talking into it. "The woman just buried her father? She's running the family ranch single-handedly and now the ex-husband is keeping her from getting her cattle to summer pasture? Of course we'll go help."

Dana hadn't been so sure that her niece should go, but Ella wasn't having any of that. She'd been riding with her cousins since college. She wasn't sitting this one out. So the three of them had packed up and headed for a small community south of Jackson Hole, Wyoming.

Angus had been looking forward to seeing Jinx

again. He remembered her red hair and her temper and was intrigued to find out what had happened to that girl. *That girl*, he'd seen tonight, had grown into a beautiful woman. Her hair wasn't quite as red, but her brown eyes still reminded him of warm honey. And those freckles… He smiled to himself. She didn't try to hide them, any more than she tried to hide the fact that she was a woman you didn't want to mess with.

For a moment earlier he'd thought that she had remembered him. But why would she? They'd just been kids, thrown together for a few hours because of their mothers.

He'd seen her looking at the scar on his chin. If anything could have jogged her memory, the scar should have, he thought as they entered the bunkhouse.

"It's more than Jinx needing wranglers to get her cattle up to summer range," Ella said quietly beside him.

He nodded, having felt it since they'd reached the ranch. Jinx had more trouble than a lack of hired help.

Back in the bunkhouse, he'd just tossed his bedroll onto the top bunk when he heard a revved engine growing louder as a vehicle approached the ranch.

"Stay here," he said to Ella, signaling to his brother to stay with her.

He picked up his weapon from the bed, strapped it on and stepped out of the bunkhouse into the darkness to see the glow of headlights headed straight for them.

JINX PICKED UP the shotgun by the front door on her way out to the porch. The moment she'd heard the engine, she'd known it was T.D. and that he was going to be a problem. By now he would have had a snoot full of beer and have worked himself up. She didn't need to see her ex-husband's pickup come to a dust-boiling stop just short of the house to know that he was in one of his moods.

The driver's-side door was flung open almost before he'd killed the engine. *Drunk again*, she thought with a silent curse. Tucker David "T.D." Sharp stumbled out of the pickup, looking nothing like the handsome, charming cowboy who'd lassoed her heart and sweet-talked her all the way to the altar.

"You get out here, JoRay!" he yelled as he stumbled toward the house. "We need to talk."

"I'm right here," she said as she stepped from the dark shadows of the porch. She saw his eyes widen in surprise—first seeing her waiting for him and then when he spotted the shotgun in her hands. "You need to leave, T.D. I've already called the sheriff."

He smirked at that. "Even if you did call him,

it will take Harvey at least twenty minutes to get out here."

"That's what the loaded shotgun is for," she said calmly, even though her heart was racing. Just seeing him in this state set her on alert. She knew firsthand what he was capable of when he got like this. He'd torn up the kitchen, breaking dishes and some of her mother's collectibles during one of his tantrums.

"Come on, JoRay. I just want to talk to you," he whined as he took another step closer. "Remember what it was like? You and me? You *loved* me. I *still* love you." He took another step. "I deserve another chance. I swear I can change."

"That's close enough." She raised the shotgun, pointing the business end of the barrel at the center of his chest.

He stopped, clearly not sure she wouldn't use it on him. She saw his expression change. "You had no business kicking me off this ranch," he said, his tone going from wheedling to angry in a heartbeat. He spat on the ground. "I got me a lawyer. Half this ranch is mine and I intend to take what's mine. This ranch and you, if I want it. You're still my wife. I can take it all." He started toward her when a voice out of the darkness stopped him.

"Not tonight you aren't."

A wrangler stepped from the shadows into the

ranch-yard light by the bunkhouse. She saw the faint gleam of the scar on his chin. She also saw that Angus was armed. He hadn't pulled his gun, but it was in sight and T.D. saw it, too.

"Who the hell are you?" her almost-ex-husband demanded.

"The lady asked you to leave," Angus said, his voice low, but forceful.

T.D. scoffed. "You going to make me?"

"If it comes to that, yes." The cowhand still hadn't moved, hadn't touched the gun at his hip, but there was something like steel in his tone.

She could see T.D. making up his mind. He'd come out here looking for a fight even if he hadn't realized it. But with T.D., like most bullies, he preferred better odds.

He swore and shot Jinx a lethal look. "This isn't over. You might have hired yourself some… cowboys," he said as some of the other wranglers came out of the bunkhouse and watched from a distance, "but when they're gone…" She heard the promised threat, saw it in his gaze. He'd be back for more than the ranch.

Jinx felt a shudder. How could she have not seen the mean side of this man before she stupidly married him? Because he'd kept it well hidden. Drunk, he was even worse, filled with an unexplained rage. She'd felt the brunt of that anger. He'd never hit her. He wasn't that stupid. But he'd beat her down with his angry words every time he drank until she'd had enough and sent him packing at gunpoint.

Her father, Ray, had been in the hospital then. Once he died, T.D. got it into his head that he deserved a second chance. When that didn't work, he'd decided the ranch should be his. And so should Jinx. He'd refused to sign the divorce papers until she settled up with him.

The problem with the man was that he never took no for an answer. Egged on by his friends he drank with and some of the other ranchers he'd grown up with who'd tried to buy her out the moment her father had died, T.D. felt both the ranch and she were his legal right.

Legally, he might have some right to the ranch, unfortunately, because they were still husband and wife technically. She hadn't had the sense to get a prenuptial agreement signed before they'd married. She'd been in love and stupid. But no matter how much of a fight T.D. put up, she was divorcing him. And while he might get his hands on half the proceeds from the ranch, he would never get his hands on her again if she could help it.

T.D. started toward his truck, stopped and tilted his head as if listening. With a smirk, he turned back to say, "If you called the sheriff, he's sure taking his time getting here." His gaze locked with hers for a moment. "Liar, liar, pants on fire, all Miss High-and-Mighty. You didn't even call the sheriff."

"If I'd called the sheriff," she said quietly, "he would have stopped me from shooting you, if you'd taken another step in my direction."

The words seemed to hit T.D. like a strong wind. He wavered, his gaze locking with hers. "So why'd you bother with a restraining order, then?" he snapped, thinking he was smarter than she was.

"Because it will look better in court after I kill you. 'I tried to keep him away, but he just wouldn't listen.'"

"Best keep it loaded and beside your bed, then," he said, smirking at her. "Because I'll be back."

She didn't doubt that. He would come back when it was just her and Max alone on the ranch. "And I'll kill you before I let you touch me again."

Her words inflamed him—just as she knew they would. But he wasn't the only one with a temper. She'd put up with all she was going to from this man. She didn't want him to doubt that she would pull the trigger on both barrels when he came back.

T.D. slammed his fist down on the hood of his pickup as he stumbled to the driver's-side door and jerked it open. He shot her a hateful look before climbing behind the wheel. The engine revved. He threw the truck in Reverse and tore off down the road, throwing dirt and gravel.

Jinx let out the breath she'd been holding. Moments before, she'd half expected T.D. to turn and charge her like a raging bull, forcing her to shoot him or pay the price for even a moment's hesitation. She figured the only reason he hadn't was because of Angus.

As she turned to thank him, she saw that the spot where he'd been standing was empty. Like the others, he must have gone back inside the bunkhouse. Apparently, he hadn't wanted or needed thanks. But now he'd put himself in the line of fire. T.D. wouldn't forget.

ANGUS STEPPED AROUND the side of the bunkhouse, listening to the sound of T.D.'s pickup engine fading in the distance. He hoped the man had enough sense not to come back, but he wouldn't bet on that.

He thought of the way that Jinx had handled the situation and he smiled. Angus had come down here believing that it was to save not just Jinx's cattle—but the woman herself.

After seeing her with that shotgun tonight, staring down her husband, Angus realized Jinx McCallahan could take care of herself. It didn't surprise him. He thought of the girl he'd met just that once. She'd made an impression on him all those years ago. She'd done it again tonight.

Her almost-ex-husband thought he could bully her. Well, T. D. Sharp had picked the wrong woman to try to intimidate. Angus could have told him that just based on knowing her a few hours years before. You didn't want to mess with that redhead, he thought, smiling to himself.

So as he stood in the dark, pretty sure T.D. wasn't headed back this way—at least not yet, he reevaluated what he was doing here. Helping Jinx get her cattle to summer range, but after that... he wasn't so sure.

Angus thought of the woman standing on the porch with the loaded double-barrel shotgun trained on her not-soon-enough-ex-husband. He realized he wasn't here to rescue her. She could rescue herself. But maybe, with some luck, he could keep her from killing T.D. and going to jail.

PATTY STOOD IN front of the bathroom mirror inspecting her throat. It was still red in spots and bruised in others. She could make out T.D.'s fingerprints where he'd choked her. She touched the spot tenderly and cursed Jinx. Just the mention of her name sent T.D. in a tailspin. Until he was done with that woman, he wasn't himself. She had to remember that.

Stepping out of the bathroom, she thought she

heard a vehicle. T.D. would come back. He'd be all apologetic and loving. He'd done it before another time when he'd gotten rough with her. And like tonight, it had been over Jinx McCallahan.

Oh, how she hated that woman, she thought, fisting her hands, fingernails biting into her palms. She'd give anything to get that woman out of their lives.

And now T.D. had gone out to her ranch to see her as if he could talk her into giving him another chance. The damned fool. It would serve him right if he got himself arrested—or shot. She wouldn't put it past Jinx to shoot him. Maybe then he'd realize that she didn't give two hoots about him.

Tears burned her eyes. What was wrong with the man? He had a woman who loved him unconditionally and still he couldn't stay away from that…ranch woman. He'd left her to go to Jinx. It burned at her insides. What if he didn't come back tonight? What if Jinx gave him a second chance? The thought made her sick to her stomach. Why couldn't she just let T.D. go?

She felt bitterness roiling in her stomach. If only Jinx would sell her ranch and leave town like most people thought she would after her father died. Let her move far away. Then T.D. would come to his senses. As long as Jinx was around, she'd keep him stirred up.

Her phone rang. For a moment she thought it would be T.D. Maybe he'd gone down to the bar and had started feeling guilty about their fight and was now calling to apologize. Or maybe invite her down to the bar to have a drink with him. Wouldn't it be something to be able to go out in public together? That would show Jinx.

She checked her cell phone, instantly disappointed. It was only Wyatt, T.D.'s friend, probably calling to ask if she knew where the man was. "Hey," she said, picking up. Maybe T.D. had asked him to call her.

"Are you all right? I saw T.D.'s truck down at the bar. Figured you'd be alone. You two have a fight?"

Patty's heart dropped. If T.D. was at the bar, then maybe he *wasn't* planning to come back tonight.

"You okay?" Wyatt asked.

She felt touched by his concern. The shy cowboy was so sweet. Too bad she couldn't fall for him instead of T.D. "Wyatt, you have to stop worrying about me." He'd found her sobbing her eyes out the last time she and T.D. had had a bad fight. He'd run a clean washcloth under the cold-water faucet in the bathroom, wrung it out and handed it to her. He'd asked if he could get her anything to eat, something to drink.

He was so thoughtful. She wished T.D. was

more like him. And while she appreciated the fact that Wyatt cared, at the same time, it felt a little creepy. Sometimes she wondered if he watched her apartment just waiting for T.D. to leave in one of his moods.

"I could come over," Wyatt said now.

She touched her throat. It still hurt. Wyatt would notice the bruises and the dark spots that looked like fingertips. "I don't think that's a good idea. You know how T.D. is. He wouldn't like it." Who was she kidding? T.D. wouldn't care.

"Was he alone at the bar?" she asked.

"I don't know. I didn't go inside. Patty, what do you see in him?"

It was a question she'd asked herself many times over the year she'd been seeing T.D. He'd never made it a secret that he loved his wife and yet, she'd been convinced that one day he would leave Jinx and marry her. Instead, Jinx had thrown him out and now T.D. was determined to get the woman back.

"I'm in love with him," she said simply. "You know that."

"I know. It's just that…he doesn't treat you right, Patty. You need a man who values you for who you are. You have so much to offer a man. A man who deserves it."

She couldn't argue that. Like tonight, she didn't need Wyatt to tell her that it was mean of T.D.

to come by only to leave right after they'd had sex. She knew he was using her and it broke her heart, but what could she do? The alternative was to not see him at all.

"You have to know how I feel about you. What can I do to show you? Just name it, Patty," Wyatt pleaded. "I would do anything for you."

She walked back into the bathroom and stared at her reflection in the mirror for a moment. Wyatt was right. She deserved better. "There *is* something you could do. Where are you now?"

"Just down the street." His voice sounded hopeful and she knew he'd meant it about doing anything for her. With a little persuasion, she thought she could get Wyatt to do the one thing she might ask.

"Come on up. But make it quick. T.D. will be coming back soon."

AFTER LEAVING THE RANCH, T.D. had considered going back to Patty's. But he wasn't up for another fight. Nor was he up for apologizing. Patty just didn't get it. He wanted Jinx, as much as he hated her right now. His wife thought she had the upper hand at the moment. Maybe she did. Maybe that was why he was so angry.

He'd driven straight to the bar, telling himself that maybe he would sneak back out to the ranch later tonight and surprise Jinx. A need stirred in him like none he'd ever felt, and he kept reminding himself that she was still his wife. She'd better not be seeing anyone else. Just the thought of that cowboy who'd come out with his six-shooter strapped on his hip...

He ordered a beer even though he could tell Marty hadn't wanted to serve him at all. But Marty also didn't want any trouble, as if he could sense that T.D. was just spoiling for a fight. It had been a long time since he'd broken up a bar.

"One beer, T.D., and then you head on home," the bartender told him.

"Home? And where exactly would that be, Marty?" he asked angrily as he picked up the cold beer the man had set in front of him. He took a long drink. It did little to cool down his fury. Jinx had no right to treat him this way. She'd made him the laughingstock of town. He couldn't let her get away with it. Half that ranch was his and damned if she wasn't going to give it to him. If she thought they were finished, then she didn't know him very well.

He smiled to himself and took another gulp of beer. From what he'd seen out at her place, she was planning to take that herd of hers into the mountains tomorrow. It would take her a few days of good weather and good luck to get them up to the high country.

T.D. had made that trip with her last year. He

knew the route she took and where she camped each night. As he finished his beer, he realized that he hadn't believed she would get anyone to help her take her cattle up to summer range. Now that she had, she'd forced his hand. He could no longer just threaten to follow her up into the mountains. He had to do it. He had to show her. And he knew just how to do it.

WYATT FELT SHAKEN to his core as he left Patty's apartment. His hands actually shook as he started his truck. On one hand, he couldn't believe his good luck. On the other... He left, driving aimlessly through town, his mind whirling.

He'd had a crush on Patty since grade school. Not that she'd ever noticed him except on those few occasions when he'd stopped into the café where she waitressed. She was nice enough then, smiling and chatting him up. He wasn't stupid. He knew she was like that with everyone because she hoped for a good tip.

Over the years, he'd watched her go through a couple of bad marriages and twice as many equally bad relationships. But nothing had cooled his ardor for her. He'd always known he was what she needed. He'd only hoped that one day she would realize it.

Now he had finally told her how he felt and to his surprise, she'd made him an offer. The offer was less than what he'd hoped for and yet more than he'd expected. He felt as if full of helium. This must be what people meant when they said they were floating on cloud nine.

Of course, there was a catch, he thought, feeling himself come back to earth with a thud.

"Word is that Jinx is driving her cattle up to summer range tomorrow," she'd said once they were seated on the couch in her living room. She'd sat so close to him that her perfume had filled his nostrils making him feel weak. He couldn't help but notice that she'd forgotten to button the two top buttons on her blouse, making it gap open. Sitting this close he could see the swell of her full breasts above her lacy black bra.

He'd also seen the red marks on her neck, a couple of them deep bruises, but he'd known better than to say anything. He'd figured it was why she'd invited him up so he waited for her to bring up the subject.

"Wyatt, you're his best friend," she'd said, leaning toward him. "You know T.D. is planning something. Once Jinx gets those cattle to the high country, T.D. will lose his leverage—or at least what he sees as leverage."

He'd nodded, surprised that Patty knew this about T.D. and yet still wanted the man. "He's threatened to follow her up into the mountains," he'd admitted. "But I think it's just talk."

She'd scoffed at that. "He'll get himself all worked up tonight after a few beers and then he'll want you and Travis to go with him since he doesn't have the guts to do it alone, and the two of you don't have the guts to turn him down."

He'd winced, knowing it was true and that she was right. He'd agree to go once T.D. started pressuring him. You just didn't say no to him, and Wyatt hadn't since they were kids growing up. T.D. had gotten him into so much trouble over the years. But like she said, the man was his best friend.

What she'd said next had floored him. "I want you to make sure that Jinx McCallahan never comes out of those mountains."

At first he'd thought he'd misunderstood her. "I don't know what you mean."

And then Patty had leaned toward him, her full breasts brushing his arm as she kissed him. "Do this for me and I promise you won't regret it." She kissed him harder, giving him a little of her tongue. He'd about lost it right there.

But when he'd reached for her, she'd pushed him away. "Not until you do me this favor." Then she'd taken his hand and put it on her warm breast. He'd felt her nipple harden under his palm. And just as quickly, she'd pulled it away. "Now you should go. You wouldn't want T.D. to catch you here."

He'd stumbled out of her apartment to his rig and started driving aimlessly. She wasn't serious about any of it, he told himself. Not the offer. Not the favor she'd made him promise to think about as he was leaving. The woman didn't realize what she was asking. Or what she was offering.

"If you and T.D. get up in those mountains trying to sabotage Jinx and her cattle drive, anything could happen," Patty had insisted as she'd walked him to the door. "Accidents happen. No one even knows who did what."

There was no mistaking what she'd asked him to do for her. Kill Jinx. As if the woman was Patty's only problem. It astounded him that she didn't know T.D. at all. Even if Jinx wasn't in the picture, T.D. wasn't going to marry her. He'd string her along until he found someone else he thought he deserved more. Then he would break her heart all over again. But this time Wyatt would be there to pick up the pieces. Unless he let Patty down now.

He saw T.D.'s pickup parked in front of the bar and their friend Travis getting out of his rig to go inside. He pulled in, honked his horn and Travis stopped to wait for him.

That he'd even given a second thought to Patty's favor was insane. He couldn't kill anyone, especially his best friend's wife, he told himself as he climbed out of his truck in the glow of the neon bar sign. Why would Patty think he was capable of such a thing?

Because she knew how much he wanted her.

Patty was the only woman in town who saw him as anything but a shy, awkward cowboy who lived with his mother when he wasn't working on some ranch or another. She was offering him something he'd only dreamed of for years. He could still taste her on his lips as he and Travis pushed into the bar.

Chapter Three

As T.D. finished his beer, he tried to understand where he'd gone wrong. Too bad his father wasn't still around. His old man would have told him how worthless he was, happily listing every mistake he'd ever made, and the list was long.

He'd thought marrying Jinx would change him. Even his father would have been surprised that a woman like Jinx would have given two cents about him, let alone married him. But now she was divorcing him, proving that his father was right. He didn't deserve Jinx. He really was worthless.

But Patty aside, he wanted to argue that he'd been a pretty good husband. Just not the one Jinx wanted. He ground his teeth at the thought. What the devil had she wanted anyway? A man she could boss around? Or one who would take over the ranch and run it the way he saw fit? He could run that ranch with one hand tied behind him— if she'd give him another chance. So he'd made a few mistakes when she'd let him run it. He wouldn't make those mistakes again.

He fumed at the thought of the way Jinx had treated him at the end. He'd looked into her beautiful face and he'd seen the disgust he'd grown up with. He wasn't good enough for her, never had been, her look said. He saw that look every night when he closed his eyes to try to sleep.

The only thing that kept him sane was drinking. If he drank enough, sometimes he'd pass out and didn't have to see that look.

"Another beer," he said, banging his empty bottle hard on the bar and getting a side-eye from the bartender.

"You've had enough," Marty said as he came down, a bar rag in his hand. He picked up the empty bottle. "I told you I was only serving you one. Why don't you call it a night, T.D.?"

"What don't you—" The rest was cut off as his two friends came in on a rush of spring air. He could see how this was going to go if he stayed. He was in one of his tear-this-place-apart moods.

"Let's get out of here," he said to his friends, sliding off his stool before they could join him. "If they don't want our business here, we'll take it somewhere else. Anyway, there's free beer at Patty's. She's a little mad at me, but I still have my key." He picked up his change, leaving no tip for Marty as he pocketed the few coins. Marty acted as if he didn't care. He seemed glad to see him go.

"Why don't we go to my place?" Travis suggested. "I've got beer and there's no one there to give us any trouble."

T.D. laughed. "Good idea. I need to let Patty wonder where I am for a few days anyway."

Outside, the cold spring night air took his breath away for a moment. Warm, summerlike weather was a good two months away in this part of Wyoming. He started toward his pickup when he spotted the sheriff standing across the street leaning on his cruiser. He swore under his breath. The SOB was just waiting for him to get behind the wheel. Harvey had been laying for him, hoping to catch him at something so he could throw his butt behind bars.

T.D. laughed. "Let's walk. It's a nice night," he said to his friends.

"Are you kidding?" Travis squawked. "It's freezing out."

"Man up," T.D. said as he gave Travis a playful shove and then the three of them were making their way down the street, leaving their vehicles parked in front of the bar. It wasn't as if they hadn't done that before on those nights when they were too drunk to drive home.

"You're awfully quiet," T.D. said, throwing his arm around Wyatt's shoulder. "I'd suspect you had woman trouble if I didn't know you better." He laughed at his own joke as Wyatt shrugged off his arm.

"I might surprise you someday," Wyatt said.

"Right," T.D. said with a chuckle. "But in all seriousness we need to talk about tomorrow. I hope you're both ready to ride up in the mountains. We've got to catch up with Jinx and do a little damage."

"What kind of damage?" Travis asked, sounding worried.

"You know," T.D. said, feeling the alcohol he'd consumed. Sometimes it made him feel invincible. He was going to show everyone, especially Jinx. "Get ready for some…high jinks."

WYATT HAD BEEN hopeful that Patty was wrong and T.D. would give up on trying to stop Jinx's cattle drive. He should have known better. T.D. was at loose ends after the breakup. One day he was determined to get her back; the next he just wanted half the ranch so he could get on with his life.

Going up into the mountains after Jinx and her herd, though, was just plain crazy. Nothing good could come of that. Someone could get killed. Wasn't that what Patty was hoping? The reminder sent a chill through him. That he would even consider her request… Was he so desperate for anything that Patty offered that he'd even consider it?

Once they reached Travis's trailer, they consumed more beer and listened to T.D.'s account of what had happened earlier tonight, first at Patty's, then out at the ranch with Jinx. Wyatt watched as T.D. worked himself up for tomorrow. Just as Patty had said, the cowboy was talking about chasing after the herd and Jinx as they headed for the high country and doing anything he could to ruin her life.

"It's time I showed Jinx what was what," T.D. blustered, fueled by the booze and the anger he had going.

"Come on, T.D., what's the point in going all the way up there after her?" Travis argued. "Sounds like it could get us all killed or thrown into jail and for what? Just to mess with your ex-wife?"

T.D. swore. "She's not my ex yet. I need to show her that I mean business. And up in the mountains, the sheriff won't be watching me like a hawk. That old fart is out to get me because of her."

Wyatt had to ask, "You got a plan?" He still held out hope that all this was just the booze talking. Maybe by morning, T.D. would be so hungover he'd have changed his mind. The thought both relieved him and upset him. He hated to think how it would disappoint Patty. Wyatt couldn't stand the thought of her thinking less of him.

T.D. grinned. "You know how dangerous a cattle drive can be. Accidents happen. And let's face it. Jinx is due for some bad luck the way I see it. She can't just toss me out without a dime. Before I'm through with her, she'll be begging me to take half the ranch. Maybe more. If something were to happen to her... Well, we're still legally married. That entire ranch could be mine...if my wife should meet with one of those accidents."

"I don't like the sound of this."

"Damn it, Travis," T.D. snapped. "Stop your whining. You don't want to come with us? Fine. Stay here and work at your old man's hardware store. Or you could tell him that you have a cattle drive to go to and won't be back for a few days."

"You're going to get me fired, T.D."

"Quit. Once I get the ranch, I can offer you a good-paying job and you won't have to put up with your old man ever again. How does that sound? You, too, Wyatt."

Wyatt couldn't imagine anything worse than working for T.D. "Sounds great," he said, which seemed to be what the cowboy needed to hear right now.

"Sure," Travis said, sounding about as enthused by the idea as he was.

He had to hand it to Travis for trying to talk sense into T.D. But ultimately, Wyatt knew that Travis would come along with them. T.D. would beat him down. Just as he would Wyatt if he'd raised objections. So he hadn't bothered, because as T.D.'s best friend, it was a foregone conclusion that he was going along.

"Then we should get some sleep," Travis said, climbing to his feet.

"Mind if I stay here, Trav?" T.D. asked as he finished his beer and stood.

"Take the guest room down the hall."

T.D. laughed. "Guest room. That broom closet of a room? You're really living large, Trav."

"I'm going home," Wyatt told the two as he got to his feet.

"I'll pick you up first thing in the morning," T.D. said. "Be ready." It wouldn't be the first time T.D. had sat outside Wyatt's mother's house, honking his horn and yelling for him to get moving.

And just as quickly, T.D. changed his mind. "Wait, first we should have one more beer to celebrate," he said, pulling Wyatt to him as Travis went to the refrigerator for the beers. "A toast to us!" he said, putting his arm around each of their shoulders. They clinked beer cans together, T.D. sloshing his own beer on the floor.

"We're going to need to pick up a few things in

the morning before we head out. I promise you, this is going to be fun," T.D. said. "Something all three of us will remember when we're old men. Isn't that right, Wyatt?" He pulled him closer.

Wyatt hoped the cowboy didn't smell Patty's perfume on him. He could still smell it on his shirt, still remember the feel of her lips and the sweet touch of her tongue in his mouth. He swallowed, afraid he couldn't do what she asked. More afraid he could.

ANGUS HADN'T SLEPT WELL. Seeing Jinx now grown-up and so beautiful and self-assured, he'd felt a sense of pride. *I knew her when*, he'd thought. But that wasn't all that stole his sleep.

Last night he'd seen how strong and capable Jinx was when facing down her soon-to-be ex-husband. He worried that if he hadn't been here, T. D. Sharp would have called her bluff and gotten killed. Unfortunately, that would have been something Jinx would have had to live with the rest of her life.

Now Angus had found himself lying awake, listening for the sound of a pickup on the road into the ranch. The one thing he'd learned about T.D. last night was that he wasn't through with Jinx and that made him dangerous—just as dangerous as the situation he, Brick and Ella had ridden into.

He must have drifted off, though, because the clang of the breakfast bell brought him up with a start. By then, Ella and Brick had been already dressed and headed for the chow hall. Angus had quickly followed. The other two wranglers had straggled into the ranch kitchen a little later.

"I'd like you to ride point with me," Jinx told him at breakfast.

"Happy to," Angus said. He and the ranch woman would be riding at the head of the line of cattle. He'd felt her studying him as if trying to understand why he seemed familiar, he figured. Maybe he'd tell her once they were alone on the cattle drive. Not that she would probably be happy to hear their first meeting story, he thought, touching his scar.

Jinx turned to Ella and Brick. "I thought the two of you could work the flank and swing positions farther back." She considered Royce and Cash. "You'll be the drag men bringing up the rear, picking up stragglers and keeping the line moving."

"Whatever you say, trail boss," Cash had said with a smirk.

Jinx seemed to ignore him. "We'll see how that works out. Max will be bringing up the rear in the chuckwagon."

At daybreak Angus and the rest of the wranglers saddled up and began to move the large herd of cattle toward the mountains. They left the valley floor for the foothills dotted with tall pines. Angus felt a sense of relief to be riding away from the ranch.

The days ahead would be filled with long hours on horseback, herding cattle up into the towering mountains of western Wyoming. He loved cattle drives and always had. It was a peaceful existence. *At least for the moment*, he thought as he looked back down the road. Soon they would start the climb up into the mountains.

He found himself looking over his shoulder, wondering how long it would be before he spotted riders coming after them. How long it would be before he saw T. D. Sharp again. By then, they would be far from civilization. They would be on their own since Jinx had said their cell phones wouldn't work until they reached the top of the mountain—and even that was sketchy.

They moved cattle all morning and now trailed them along a creek through the pines. Cattle tended not to trail in a group, but string out in a long line. There were natural leaders who would take their places in front, while all the rest trailed behind. A head of a thousand could stretch out a mile or two so the wranglers worked in pairs on each side of the line.

The day had broken clear and sunny, reminding Angus how much he loved this work. He breathed in the spring air, rich with sweet pine, the scent of bright green spring grasses. It mixed with the scent of dust and cattle on the warm breeze. He lived for this and couldn't imagine any other life, he thought as he turned his face up to the sun. He knew his mother hoped that one day he would return and help run Cardwell Ranch in the Gallatin Canyon near Big Sky, Montana.

Lately, the ranch had been calling him. He could feel his time of being a saddle tramp was almost over. He just wasn't sure his brother Brick realized it. Or how his cousin Ella would take the news. Knowing her, she had already sensed his growing need to return home.

He'd grown up on Cardwell Ranch, fished the blue ribbon trout stream of the Gallatin, skied Lone Peak and ridden through the mountains on horseback from the time he could sit a saddle. But as he took in this part of Wyoming, he thought nothing could be more beautiful than its towering snowcapped peaks.

His gaze shifted to the woman who rode opposite him. He could see her through the tall pines. Like him, she, too, was smiling. "Beautiful, isn't it?" she called to him as if sensing him watching her.

"Sure is." Jinx in her element was more beautiful than the country around her. Her long, copper-colored hair was tied off low on the back of her neck. Her straw cowboy hat was pushed back and her freckled face turned up to the morning sun making her brown eyes sparkle. He couldn't help staring.

At a sound behind him, he turned as his brother rode up, all smiles. "You have a nice herd here," Brick called to Jinx. "Excuse me for saying it, but you look real pretty this morning." With that he spurred his horse before he turned back to his flank position.

Angus rolled his eyes at him and rode off to pick up one of the cows that had wandered off, before falling back into line. He saw that Jinx had dropped back to say something to Brick and shook his head. His brother. If there was a pretty woman around, Brick was going to try to charm her.

But Angus suspected his brother was wasting his time. Jinx had already fallen for one cowboy whom she was now trying to get rid of. He didn't think she was in the market for another.

ELLA SAW THE exchange and chuckled to herself. Her cousins were so competitive that her aunt Dana said they had probably arm wrestled in the womb. Ella wouldn't have been surprised. She'd grown up with the two of them always trying to outdo each other as boys and now as men—especially for the attention of women.

She wasn't worried this time, though. Jinx, she suspected, could see through anything the two did to impress her. She just hoped they all knew it was only for fun. Maybe she needed to remind Angus of that, though. She'd seen the way he had looked at Jinx earlier this morning. It surprised her and worried her a little.

Right now both Jinx and Angus were vulnerable. Jinx, because of her father's death and her upcoming divorce. Angus, because he'd finally gotten over his heartbreak from the last woman he'd fallen for and he now exhibited signs of a growing restlessness. She suspected he would be returning to Cardwell Ranch soon to stay.

Ella turned in her saddle to look back, making sure they hadn't lost any cattle. In the distance she could see the chuckwagon bouncing up the trail behind a team of two horses with Max at the reins. Closer, Royce and Cash were riding next to each other, appearing deep in conversation. As if sensing her watching them, they separated to move some of the slower cattle up into the line.

She didn't like the vibes she picked up from the two men and planned to sleep with her sidearm handy. She'd been a little surprised that Jinx had taken them on. But the ranch woman was desperate or Ella and her cousins wouldn't be here.

"First cattle drive with a woman wrangler," Royce said as he rode up next to her. But when he saw Jinx riding in their direction, he pretended to turn back to look for cattle.

"Doing all right?" Jinx asked her as she brought her horse alongside Ella's.

"Just fine."

Jinx rode astride her for a few minutes. "You let me know if anyone bothers you."

Ella laughed. "I can handle myself."

"I don't doubt that. But there's two of them and I don't trust either of them, do you?"

"No. Don't worry. I've been keeping an eye on them. I'm not sure why, but I don't expect them to stay with us long."

"Funny you should say that. They both hit me up for an advance on their wages before we left this morning," Jinx said. "I turned them down, but I suspect I'll be paying them off before we ever reach summer range."

If that was the worst they could expect, Ella thought. They rode along for a few minutes, the herd of cattle a rust-colored mass of slow movement. "I heard about your father," Ella said without looking at the woman. "I'm sorry."

She felt Jinx's surprised gaze on her for a long moment before the woman said, "I wondered how much you all knew about my...situation." Ella said nothing. "I suppose it's no secret that my mother and Dana Cardwell Savage were friends." Ella knew that the two women had met at cattlewomen conferences and stayed in touch until Jinx's mother's death. "I suspect that's why the three of you showed up on my ranch."

Ella kept silent, riding along through the spring morning, glad, though, that Jinx knew. She didn't like keeping anything from the woman. She liked Jinx.

"I guess what I'm saying is that I appreciate you being here, but it could get...dangerous."

Ella looked over at her and smiled. "Then I'm glad we're here to help."

The ranch woman chuckled at that. "We'll see how you feel when the shooting starts—so to speak."

She met the woman's gaze. "We know what we're up against. We didn't come into this blind."

"I just hope you don't regret it." With that, Jinx rode off.

STILL HALF-DRUNK AND sound asleep in Travis's spare bedroom, T.D. came awake with a start at the sound of someone banging hard on the door.

"Tucker David Sharp, we know you're in there," a deep male voice called from outside.

He froze, wondering how they'd found him. He considered going out the only window large enough that he could fit through. Then he swore under his breath, realizing that going out the window wasn't going to help. He needed to try to settle this and hope for the best.

"Give me a minute," he called as he rolled over to look at his cell phone. He couldn't believe he'd slept so late. He swung his legs over the side of the bed and put his throbbing head in his hands. The cattle drive. Jinx would have been up before first light. Who knew how far she'd managed to get by now. Cussing his hangover along with his bad luck, he wondered when his fortune would change. Trouble just seemed to dog him.

"Goin' to bust down the door if you don't open it," said the voice on the other side.

"What's going on?" Travis asked from the spare room doorway. "You know this guy?"

Pushing past Travis, he said over his shoulder, "Don't worry. I'll take care of it." In the living room, T.D. took a deep breath, let it out and stumbled to the door.

The man standing outside was big and beefy with a bulldog face and dark eyes as hard and cold as a gravestone.

"Shawn, come in," T.D. said as the man pushed his way in sans an invitation. He closed the door and turned to face him, a little surprised that Shawn had come alone. Little did he doubt that there were more men, probably waiting in the car in case T.D. caused any trouble. "Look, I know I owe you money."

The man laughed, setting his jowls in motion. He stopped abruptly to narrow those death-like eyes on him. "You *owed* money. Now it is past due. Perhaps you didn't read the fine print when you took out the loan."

"This is a small town so I assume you know what's happened to me." He waited for Shawn to say something. When he didn't, T.D. continued even though he knew his words were falling on deaf ears. "My wife is divorcing me. I have a lawyer who says I can get half of her ranch. You know the spread, so you know how much money we're talking about here. So it shouldn't be that long before I'll have what I owe."

Shawn smiled at that. "Don't forget interest and the late fee that is added every day you don't pay. But here's the problem. My boss doesn't want to wait."

T.D. remembered his father's expressions when bill collectors came around. *They can't eat you.* But they darned sure could mess you up. *Can't get blood out of a turnip.* Another of his father's expressions. But Shawn wasn't your normal bill collector. It was T.D.'s blood that was going to run free if he didn't come up with a plan and quickly.

And it wasn't as if he'd taken out a loan at the bank. He'd gambled on being able to pay what he owed, just as he'd gambled away any money he could get his hands on. "Five thousand. I can get you that by the end of the week."

Shawn raised a brow. "You don't have two nickels to rub together. Where will you get five grand?"

"Leave that to me. One week. Five thousand to hold your boss until I can pay him everything I owe him."

"With interest and late fees."

"Right," T.D. said, thinking how large a chunk that was going to take out of his half of the ranch. But when he considered the alternative, what choice did he have? Jinx had no idea just how deep his gambling debts had gotten. Not that she was going to bail him out again. She'd made that clear before she'd thrown him out.

His future looked bleak. Unless he got the entire ranch. Like he'd told his friends, anything could happen on a cattle drive.

Chapter Four

The day passed in a blur for Angus as they worked the cattle up through the pines and began the long climb to the high mountain range. Saddle sore after eating the dust the cattle kicked up, they had stopped midday for a quick lunch and to let the cattle drink from the stream. Then it was back in the saddle. Jinx had said she wanted to make it up to the old corrals the first day so they pushed ahead and reached the spot by the time the light began to fade.

Angus climbed off his horse now to close the gate to the corral that held the horses. The herd lowed from a large vibrant green meadow, the cattle glowing in the last of the day's light.

He felt the hours in a saddle. But it was a nice tired feeling of accomplishment. Also, he was thankful that they'd gotten the herd this far without any trouble. He'd actually been a little surprised. But then again, T. D. Sharp might be the kind of man who made threats when he was drinking, then didn't follow through on them.

At least he hoped that was the case. He'd seen Jinx watching the trail behind them. She expected her ex to make trouble. But they'd been moving at a pretty good pace all day. He figured T.D. would wake up with a hangover this morning and not be anxious to jump on a horse and head for the hills.

But Angus didn't doubt that the man wasn't through making trouble for her. He just didn't know how or when the cowboy would strike, only that he would if he could get some friends together to buoy his confidence. Angus had met men like him before.

All day he'd kept an eye on Jinx—as well as Royce and Cash. He'd seen Jinx's expression when she'd hired the two. She'd hesitated more with Royce and Cash than she had with Ella. That told him a lot. She didn't trust them and neither did he.

After unsaddling his horse, he left it in the fenced enclosure and headed for the chuckwagon, following the smell of something good cooking. He could see flames rising from a large campfire not far from the wagon where Max was dishing up dinner. There was steak, potatoes and beans with fresh homemade sourdough bread to soak up every bite.

Angus took his plate over to the fire, pulled up a log and sat down next to Ella and Brick.

"Good grub," Brick said as he cleaned his plate and went back for more.

Royce and Cash were still taking care of their horses. Angus didn't see Jinx. Max was busy in his wagon kitchen slopping more beans and potatoes on Brick's plate along with another steak.

"How are you doing?" Angus asked Ella quietly. He knew she never complained and that she could hold her own. He also trusted her instincts. She had a sixth sense about some things, especially people. But sometimes he worried about her. She would get quiet and he'd know that something was bothering her. Like now.

"I'm doing better than your brother," she joked. "He is getting nowhere with Jinx."

He smiled and shook his head, letting her deflect his question for the moment. "You know Brick. He'll keep trying."

"She likes you, though," Ella said, glancing over at him. "She isn't sure she can trust you, though. I've seen her watching you and frowning."

Angus chuckled, knowing trust wasn't the problem. But he said, "I would imagine she won't be trusting any man for some time to come. However, I asked how you were doing."

Ella smiled, but it didn't quite reach her eyes. "I'm fine."

"Well, if you want to talk about it…" He let that hang, seeing that whatever seemed to be bothering her, she wasn't ready to share it.

Over by the chuckwagon, Brick had struck up a conversation with Jinx as she came to get her plate. Ella shook her head as she and Angus watched him. "She sees right through him and yet he still thinks he can charm his way into her good graces. You, however, haven't tried to charm her."

"Nor am I going to try." Jinx wasn't like the other women he and Brick met. He wasn't interested in making it a competition. The other women had recognized it as a game and had enjoyed the attention. But none of the other women were Jinx.

He ate and watched the flames rising into the wide-open sky overhead. It wouldn't be full dark for another hour or so, but by then, he figured most everyone would be out for the night except for those assigned to stand watch over the herd.

"I'm worried about Royce and Cash," he said. "You let me know if they give you any trouble."

Ella chuckled. "You sound like Jinx. But like I told her, I can take care of myself."

"I'll still be watching them both," he said and followed her gaze to where the two men had finally finished putting their horses and tack away by the old corral. Rising, he took his cousin's empty plate and his own and started toward the chuckwagon.

Brick was headed back to the campfire and stopped him. "We made good time today, don't you think?" his brother said. "Another couple of days and we'll be in the high country." Brick looked toward the towering peaks, dark against the fading light. "This job isn't going to last that long. I was thinking we could still go north for the summer and work that ranch up by the border."

Angus laughed and shook his head. "You know you aren't serious about that woman up there."

Brick cut his eyes to him. "Who says I have to be serious?" Jinx had been talking to Max at the chuckwagon, but now made her way toward them and the campfire. Brick had seen her, too.

Angus grabbed his arm to detain him for a moment. "I'd tell you that you're wasting your time but that would only make you more determined," he said with a sigh. "Emotionally, Jinx is no place good right now. The last thing she needs is a wolf like you tracking her. In case you care, I'm not interested in her so let's not make this a contest."

Brick grinned at him. "Nice speech, my brother. But I've seen the way you look at her."

"I'm worried about her and what T. D. Sharp is going to do next. You should be, too, since the man is dangerous."

"You're just *worried* about her." His brother

laughed. "I turn on the charm and get nowhere while you just quietly worry. I've also seen the way she watches you. Come on, we've been doing this since grade school." He glanced toward Jinx, who'd stopped to turn back to say something to Max. "But you should know. I could be serious about a woman like Jinx."

Angus shook his head and muttered, "I knew I was wasting my breath. You aren't serious about this woman or even the one up on the Canadian border and we both know it. Leave Jinx alone." With that he turned and walked over to the wagon where Max was watching Brick get a log for Jinx by the fire. What made him angry wasn't even his brother, but the surge of jealousy he'd felt.

"She forgot her bread," Max said, more to himself than Angus.

"I can take it to her."

Max studied him for a moment before handing him the plate with the bread on it. As he handed over his dishes and walked back to the camp-fire, he thought about how protective Max was of Jinx. The woman seemed to bring that out in all of them. He reminded himself that this was just a job, even though he knew it wasn't. They were here because Jinx needed their help and not just with her cattle, he feared. But his cousin and brother were right about one thing. He was determined to protect Jinx, for old times' sake, he told himself. It was more than a job for him.

"Happy with the progress we made today?" he asked Jinx as he handed her the plate of bread Max had sent for her.

Jinx took a piece and he set the plate down on a spare log and sat across the fire from her. Brick had taken a log between the women.

"We're on schedule but last I heard there's supposed to be thunderstorms tomorrow," she said. "We won't be able to get any cell phone service until we get to the top of the mountain, so there is no checking to see if the storm has been upgraded or not." She sighed. "Spring in the mountains. I'm hoping we can beat the bad weather to the next large meadow where we have another corral at least for the horses."

She took a bite of her meal. Angus suspected she didn't even taste it. A lot was riding on getting the cattle to summer range. But he knew it was also a distraction from what had been happening down in the valley with her ex.

"That's why I want to leave at daybreak. To get as far as we can before the bad weather hits us," Jinx was saying. "If you could let the others know?"

"I'd be happy to," Angus said. He could tell that she was exhausted from more than the cattle drive. He wished there was something he could say to make things better for her, but unlike his brother, he thought Jinx probably needed silence over sweet words.

"I'll go tell Cash and Royce," he said and rose.

"Tell them chow's on, too," Max called as Angus headed over to where the men were standing and talking next to the corral holding the horses. He felt every mile in the saddle as he stretched his long legs. Walking through the tall green grass, he found himself looking forward to turning in early. They'd gotten through the first day without any trouble. No disgruntled almost-ex-husband. But a thunderstorm could change all that. Lightning was the major cause of stampedes on cattle drives.

Even if T. D. Sharp didn't show his face, they were in for a rough day tomorrow.

JINX WATCHED ANGUS GO. She still hadn't figured out why he seemed so familiar. Nor had he said anything. She sighed and rose to take her dishes back to Max.

"I can take those for you," Brick said, shooting to his feet.

She smiled but shook her head. "Stay here by the fire with Ella." She was glad when he sat back down. She needed to be alone. Brick was sweet and a good wrangler. He amused her with his blatant attempts to charm her, but he was wasting his time. While he resembled his brother, they didn't seem to be anything alike. Angus was a mystery to her.

The more she was around him, the more she felt a strange sense that they'd been here before. She couldn't shake the feeling that she knew this man, as in another life. It was crazy. Sometimes she'd find herself studying his face as if a memory was so close she could almost touch it.

"He's handsome, isn't he?" Max asked, startling her. She hadn't realized that she'd reached the chuckwagon. Her mind had been miles away.

"Pardon?" she asked, turning to face him as she conjured up her most innocent face.

Max laughed. "You were staring at Angus Savage—and not for the first time, I might add."

"I don't know what you're talking about. I was...thinking."

"*Thinking*? I can just imagine." He turned back to his cooking.

She didn't want to know what he'd imagined. Nor did she want to continue this conversation. Still, she asked, "Have you ever run across someone you felt as if you knew in another life?"

He chuckled. "That your story?"

"I'm serious."

Max turned to look at her. "I can see that. I suppose it's possible the two of you met before. Your mother and his were good friends." The cook frowned. "I think she took you with her up to Cardwell Ranch once years ago." So that could have been it, she thought. "You don't remember?"

She shook her head and yet as he said it, she had an image come to mind of mountains shooting up from a green river bottom and a large red barn set against a wall of rock and pine trees. A memory teased at her. "How old would I have been?"

"Eight or nine," he said as he turned back to his cleaning up. "You didn't stay long, just overnight, I think. That's probably why you don't remember."

But she did remember a little. Now it really nagged at her. It wasn't just that she'd seen him before. She couldn't shake the feeling that something had happened during that visit; she was sure of it.

She turned to look at Angus again. He'd rejoined his brother and cousin on a log by the fire. His face shone in the campfire light. Max was right about one thing; the cowboy was handsome as sin. Had he remembered her? He would have been a little older than she was by a couple of years at least.

"Why don't you just ask him?" Max said with a laugh. "Otherwise, it's going to drive you crazy."

He was right about that, as well, but what if Angus didn't remember her? She'd feel foolish.

Then again, what if he did? What if he was just waiting for her to say something?

"While you're making up your mind, why don't you hand me your dishes?" Max said with a shake of his head as he took them from her.

Leaving camp, she checked the cattle, glad that Brick and Royce had volunteered to take the first shift. She didn't expect trouble. Not tonight. T.D. was angry and vengeful, but he never planned ahead. He knew she was taking the herd up into the high country for summer grazing today. Maybe he would even wait until she returned to continue threatening her, rather than try to catch them. His laziness might pay off for her.

But unfortunately, she also knew that her being up here in the mountains put her at a disadvantage. T.D. wasn't stupid. He would realize how vulnerable she was up here. Anything could happen in the mountains on a cattle drive. People got injured. Others died. And T.D. was desperate to get his hands on her ranch. He would come after her.

In the distance she heard a coyote howl. Another answered, then another. She was more worried about wolves and bears, than coyotes. But she could only protect her herd so much. It was the nature of the business.

The camp was quiet as she walked back toward the fire. From out of the dark shadows, she spotted a lone figure still illuminated in the flames. Ella gave her a nod as she pulled up the log next to her again. The heat of the blaze felt good this high in the mountains since it was only early June.

Jinx could feel the long day in the saddle in her muscles. She yearned for sleep, but it had been hard to come by for some time now. It wasn't just T.D. who haunted her dreams. She didn't want to think about any of that. Instead, she was curious about this young woman and her lifestyle.

"If you don't mind me asking, why this life?" she asked after a few moments.

Ella smiled. "Probably same as you. I was born into it. When you're raised on a ranch, you do what you know." She shrugged. "I like what I do."

"But you aren't working your home ranch."

She shook her head almost wistfully. "It would have been too easy just to stay there. But I wasn't ready to settle down. I wanted to experience other places, other people. It's tougher as a woman to find that kind of freedom. That's why traveling with my cousins works. They give me space. I give them space."

Jinx looked toward where Angus had spread out his bedroll in the fallen dried pine needles beneath a stand of pines some distance away. "They seem nice enough," she joked.

Ella chuckled. "They'll grow on you."

"That's what I'm afraid of," Jinx said.

"Brick can be a little much."

The ranch woman shook her head. "He doesn't bother me. Has he ever been serious about a woman?"

"Not to my knowledge," Ella said. "A sure sign of fear of intimacy, huh?"

She waited a beat before she asked, "And Angus?"

"Oh, he's been in love. Got kicked in the teeth not all that long ago, so he's gun-shy."

"Aren't we all?" Jinx considered the young woman. "What about you?"

"If you're asking if I've ever met someone who made me want to settle down..." Ella shook her head. "By my age my mother had been married a few times. I'm hoping I'm a whole lot pickier than she was."

"Sorry. I didn't mean to pry. I thought everyone met someone, got married, lived happily-ever-after. That's what my parents did. They were high school sweethearts. That was the kind of marriage I'd wanted. The kind I'd just assumed I would have."

"Everyone makes mistakes when it comes to love. I'm sure I will, too."

Jinx eyed the woman, thinking how much she liked her. If they didn't live in different states, miles from each other, they could be good friends. She was going to be sorry to see Ella go when the job was over. "You seem like a woman with her head squarely set on her shoulders."

Ella laughed. "Maybe. At least when it comes to some things. I've seen my cousins make fools out of themselves over love. I swear I'm not going to do it, but then again no man has ever swept me off my feet. I've seen what love has done to some of my seemingly normal friends, as well."

Jinx knew the woman was trying to make her feel better. Just talking to her did. She stared into the flames, letting them lull her for a while before she pushed to her feet. She had no idea what tomorrow would bring other than thunderstorms, but she needed to at least try to sleep.

"You'll put the fire out?" Ella nodded. "Sleep well. We leave again at daybreak." With that, she turned and left.

The weight of the job ahead and the day in the saddle pressed on her. Taking her bedroll Jinx found herself a spot some distance from the others. Spreading it out, she lay down and stared up at the night sky through the pine boughs. She'd never seen so many stars—even back at the ranch—as she did up here. Breathing in the last scent of the campfire and the pines, she closed her eyes. She found herself smiling, glad she'd hired on the Savage brothers and their cousin Ella.

Exhausted, she fell asleep, only to be awakened to what sounded like gunfire and yelling.

Chapter Five

Angus woke to what he soon recognized as the banging of pots and pans, followed by cussing. He sat up abruptly, afraid T.D. had found their camp already. He turned in the direction of the racket. Through dawn's thin haze he saw Max standing next to the chuckwagon, his shoulders hunched in anger, a large dented pan in one hand and a huge spoon in the other. He was beating the bottom of the pot and staring off into the trees. What the—

Rolling out of his sleeping bag, Angus pulled on his boots and strapped on his gun, then headed for Max. "What happened?"

"The son of a bee broke into the wagon, made a mess and took most of our food," Max said, toning down his cursing as Jinx quickly joined them.

"Who broke into the chuckwagon?" she asked, sounding as confused by what she'd awakened to as he'd been.

Max huffed. "Dang black bear. Made a hell of a mess. I heard someone moving around in the wagon." Max slept under the wagon, but was clearly a heavy sleeper. "I looked in half-asleep and there are these red eyes staring out at me. 'Bout scared me out of my wits."

Angus chuckled and relaxed. He'd been afraid it was T.D. or someone in camp who'd gotten into their food.

"I thought you kept the food up so the bears couldn't get into it?"

"Had it locked up, but these bears… Smart as whips. Figured out how to get into the container, I guess. I should have hoisted it up in a tree, but I thought for sure it was safe in the metal box."

"How bad is it?" Jinx asked.

"You mean other than the mess?" Max rubbed his grizzled jaw for a moment. "Bear got all the meat. I'd say that was enough, wouldn't you? We have at least two more days up here before we head back. It can't be done on empty stomachs."

"Can we make do with what the bear didn't get?" she asked quietly as if not wanting the whole camp to know about this.

Angus figured it was too late for that given the racket Max had made. He could tell that the older man was still shaken by coming face-to-face with the bear. As he looked over his shoulder, he saw Brick and Ella were headed this way.

Max stared at the ground for a moment. Angus could tell that the bear had startled the cook. Max had scared it away by banging the spoon on the bottom of the pan—which now looked like the surface of the moon.

"We still have flour and sugar, salt and lard." Max raised his head. "I hope you like biscuits."

"I *love* biscuits," Angus said. "Also, I can get a couple of blue grouse and my cousin Ella is one hell of a fisherwoman." He turned and caught Ella's eye. She nodded and turned back to her gear. If he knew her, she'd have some fish from the creek for Max to fry in minutes. "We'll be fine," he said, turning back to Jinx and Max. "It's only a few days."

"Three to get back out of the mountains." Jinx smiled at him and mouthed "Thank you," before turning her attention to Max again. "We'll make do."

Max nodded sullenly. Clearly, he hated being outwitted by a bear. Not to mention the rude awakening he'd had. Jinx was also visibly upset about the loss of the food, but she appeared to be holding it in as if afraid that letting it out would only make things worse.

"Get some breakfast going," Jinx said. "I'll get the others up. If they aren't already." As she started to walk away, she touched Angus's arm. "Can I speak to you for a moment?"

He followed her away from the chuckwagon and Max for a short distance before she stopped and turned to him. "A *bear*." She shook her head as if relieved it hadn't been T.D. "Sure gave Max a scare." She let out a huff of a laugh. "I had expected trouble but I figured it would come from T.D. and his buddies." She sobered. "I know him. He won't be far behind, though. Still, my first thought was that maybe Cash or Royce was behind it. Maybe T.D. didn't put them up to hiring on with me. Maybe I'm just overly suspicious now."

Angus nodded. "You're not."

"I should send them packing right now." She met his gaze. "Problem is, we could use them. Especially with thunderstorms coming today. We only have two more days before we reach the high country if nothing slows us down."

"If you're asking my advice, I'd keep them where we can see them until then."

Jinx sighed and smiled. "I was and you're right. Fine, but I'll be watching them."

"You won't be alone," he said and walked back to where Max was still swearing as he stood looking at the mess in the wagon. "Let me help with breakfast."

The older man turned to stare pointedly at him. "You ever cooked on the trail?"

"I have," Angus said. "You want me to make the biscuits or the fire?"

Max's face broke into a grin. "We got trouble

enough without you making the biscuits, son. See to the fire." He climbed back into the wagon, mumbling to himself.

"I make some damned fine biscuits, I'll have you know," Angus called after the cook. Inside the wagon, Max huffed, but he was no longer cussing.

Angus smiled as he set about making the fire. Brick joined him. Ella had gone down to the stream. She always carried fishing line and had a knack for catching things. Angus figured it was her infinite patience. Brick went to help Max clean up the mess the bear had made.

When he had the fire going, he looked up and caught Jinx watching him.

AFTER A BREAKFAST of fried trout and biscuits, they rounded up the cattle and traveled higher into the mountains. Ella had proven her skill at catching pan-size trout. This morning he and Brick cleaned them before turning them over to Max, who dusted them with flour and dropped them in sizzling lard.

"Good breakfast," Jinx had said as she finished hers and thanked Ella for the fish before her gaze shifted to Royce and Cash. "I'd like the two of you to ride pickup again today. Keep an eye out for stragglers. If the thunderstorm is bad, I'll need you to help keep the herd from spooking."

Both men nodded. Angus had noticed that
Royce and Cash had eaten plenty of fish and biscuits. There was nothing wrong with their appe-
tites. What did surprise him was that they hadn't
asked about the ruckus this morning, keeping to
themselves as usual. He found that strange. Also
suspicious. He wondered if there was a reason
the bear had been able to get into their supplies
so easily. The men made him nervous, just like
they did Jinx and Ella.

But after breakfast and the excitement of having a bear in camp, they'd gotten a fairly early
start, riding out as they had the day before. The
sun rose and moved lazily across the canopy of
sky above the treetops.

As the morning and early afternoon slipped
away, the sun began its descent into a horizon
filled with gunmetal-gray storm clouds.

Just as Jinx had predicted, a thunderstorm was
headed their way. Angus could hear the low rumble in the distance. He rode over to join her. "How
far to the next corrals?"

She shook her head as she glanced at the storm
moving toward them. "We can't make it in time.
There's a large meadow a half mile from here.
I don't think we have a choice but to try to hold
them there."

As Angus rode point again on his side of the
herd, he saw Jinx riding back to give the others

the news. He could feel the electricity in the air. It made the hair quill on the back of his neck. He could smell the scent of rain.

Behind him, he felt the lightning strikes growing closer along with the thunder and rain as he found the meadow and circled back to help with the herd. He knew what could happen if even a few of the cattle spooked and took off. He'd seen a herd stampede in a thunderstorm and knew that was Jinx's greatest fear.

Or maybe her greatest fear was what T.D. might do if he'd decided to follow them into the mountains. If T.D. took advantage of the thunderstorm to hit just then, Angus doubted they could keep the herd from stampeding.

PATTY HAD BEEN so sure that T.D. would have come by her apartment last night—if he wasn't in jail. She needed to know what had happened so she dressed in her uniform for work, but left early so she could stop by T.D.'s favorite bar.

Sliding onto a stool down the bar from several regulars having their morning coffee, she asked Marty if he'd seen T.D. last night. She and Marty had gone to school together. He was older and had married young. He had three kids and another on the way with his wife of many years.

She'd always liked him. Always thought how

different her life would have been if she'd married someone like him and now had a home and kids.

Marty poured her a fountain cola and set it down on a napkin in front of her before he answered. "He was here. I let him have one beer and then asked him to leave. From the marks on your neck, I probably don't have to tell you that he was in one of his moods."

Self-consciously, she touched her neck. She'd thought she'd covered the worst of it with makeup. "Did he say where he was going when he left?"

"Yeah, he wrote down his entire itinerary for me." He shook his head. "He left with his minions, Wyatt and Travis."

Well, at least he hadn't been thrown in jail after going out to Jinx's ranch. Maybe she hadn't called the law on him. Or maybe he'd changed his mind and hadn't gone. Maybe he'd just come here to the bar.

She took a sip of her cola. "So you don't know where they went after they left? T.D. didn't say what his plans were?" She had to get to work soon, but first she had to know if T.D. had mentioned going after Jinx.

Marty seemed to study her for a moment. "They stopped in this morning for…supplies for a trip. They were all in T.D.'s truck with a horse trailer and three horses in the back. I would imagine you know as well as I do where they're headed." Marty leaned toward her on the bar, his gaze locking with hers. "Why do you waste your time on him?"

She chuckled and looked away, embarrassed. "I need something to do while I'm waiting for you to ask me out."

"I'm married, but I know that's like bear bait for you." Marty shook his head. "Patty, I'm serious. You're better than T.D., better than any of the men I've seen you…date. Come on, Patty, wise up. There are some good men out there. Try one of them for a change."

She put down her glass of cola a little too hard, splashing some out onto the bar. "We all can't be like you, Marty," she snapped. "In a dead-end job, with a mortgage on your double-wide and a bunch of kids."

He sighed. "Sorry, you're right. It's none of my business and what do I know anyway, right? But I'm happy, Patty. Are you?" He turned to go down the bar.

"I'm sorry. Marty? *Marty!*" But he kept walking. What made it worse was that she knew he was right. She thought her problem was Jinx. Or that her problem was T.D. She knew it was her and always had been. She was like her mother. She always went for the lowest denomination when it came to men. But that didn't mean she loved T.D. any less.

As she finished her cola and left Marty a tip, she felt her chest tighten as she thought about what she'd asked Wyatt to do. Too late to change anything, she told herself. Wyatt probably couldn't do it anyway.

For a moment, though, she felt the enormity of what she might have put into motion. She'd known Wyatt'd had a crush on her for years. She'd seen it in those puppy dog eyes of his and the way he shuffled his boots, dropping his gaze to them when he was around her, as if half-afraid to meet her eyes.

Until last night. It did amaze her how easy it had been to seduce him. All it had taken was one kiss and he'd been ready to do anything for her. He hadn't said he'd do it, though. He might chicken out. But at least she'd put the notion into his head and had given him a taste—so to speak—of the payoff if he did it.

Now, though, she felt nervous and worried. She told herself that what was done was done. Too late for second thoughts since there was nothing she could do about it. And if something did happen up there in the mountains and Jinx didn't return… Well, T.D. would be free of Jinx—and he'd have the ranch. And he'd have Patty to thank for it.

Sheriff Harvey Bessler pushed through the door as she was leaving. "Patty," he said. "I'm hoping I heard wrong." She had no desire to talk to him. Also, she was running late for work. But he was blocking the door.

"Sorry?" She made a point of looking at her phone to show him that she was on her way to work—that was if he didn't notice the waitress uniform she was wearing.

"I heard T.D. and his buddies have gone up into the mountains. But you wouldn't know anything about that, right?"

She shook her head. "Did you ask his wife?"

Harvey gave her a sad smile. "I hope he's smart enough not to go after Jinx and make trouble."

Patty glanced again at her phone. "I wouldn't know, Sheriff, but if you don't move I'll be late for work. I'd hate to tell Cora that I was late because of you. Who knows what she'd put in your food the next time you come into the café."

He sighed and stepped aside. "You have a good day, Patty."

"I'm going to try, Sheriff." As she stepped out of the bar, she saw the dark clouds moving swiftly across the valley. She glanced toward the mountains where by now T.D. would be. The air smelled of rain and the wind had picked up, swirling dust up from the gutter to whirl around her. She shielded her eyes, Marty's words still stinging her.

As the first drops began to splash down, she

made a run for the café wondering where T.D., Wyatt and Travis were right now. She knew it was too early, but she couldn't help wondering if maybe Wyatt might already have Jinx in his sights.

Chapter Six

Lightning splintered the sky in a blinding flash. Thunder followed on its heels, a boom that seemed to shake the earth under their feet.

Angus pulled on his slicker to ride the perimeter of the herd. He could feel the wind at the front of the storm kicking up. The pine trees swayed, creaking and moaning as dust devils whirled around him.

Clouds moved in, taking the light with them as the sky blackened. It was like someone had thrown a cloak over them, snuffing out the light, going from day to night. In a lightning strike, he saw the woods illuminated for a moment in sharp relief before going dark again.

When the rain came, it slashed down horizontally in hard, huge drops that pelted him and cascaded off the brim of his Stetson. Through the downpour, he could barely see Jinx on the other side of the herd, running point. He watched as the cattle began to shift restlessly. It wouldn't take much for them to panic. All it would take was for a few of them to take off at a run and spook the others and soon they would all be stampeding.

The wind tore at the trees, ripping off pieces of the boughs and sending them airborne. The rain fell in sheets, obliterating everything. A bolt of lightning zigzagged down in a blinding path in front of him. His horse reared and he had to fight to stay in the saddle as thunder exploded directly overhead in a boom that set some of the cattle at the edge of the storm running.

The herd was already jumpy. It wouldn't take much to set off more of the cattle. Too many of them running would be impossible for the two of them to turn by themselves. They would be caught in the stampede.

Angus spurred his horse as he went after them, hoping to cut them off and turn them back before the others began to move. He rode blind, the rain painful as it pelted him. The wind lay over the grass in front of him, moving like ocean waves in an angry sea.

He turned the handful of spooked cattle, steering them back toward the herd. As he did, he spotted Jinx through the rain. She and her horse appeared almost ghostlike in a lightning flash. She'd ridden out and had turned the others. The rain was so loud that when it suddenly stopped, he felt as if he'd gone deaf.

He looked over at Jinx. She sat on her horse, glancing around as surprised as he was. Just as quickly, it began to hail. Ice pellets the size of quarters fell in a wall of white that blotted out everything. He ducked his head to it, the noise as deafening as the thunder and rain had been. The hail pummeled him and the side of the mountain, quickly covering the ground and the backs of the cattle.

He rode his horse under a high, large pine tree to wait out the hailstorm. As he did, he could hear the lightning and thunder moving off over the mountains. It wasn't until the hail began to let up, that he saw Jinx again. She sat astride her horse under a pine tree only yards away. He saw the relief on her face.

More than relief. She smiled with the kind of joy that comes with knowing you made it through something challenging. He returned her smile as he took off his hat and shook off the melting hailstones. The herd stood, backs coated white, the storm over. Angus settled his Stetson back on his head and felt himself relax a little as droplets of moisture fell from the sodden pines as the storm moved on as quickly as it had appeared.

WYATT WATCHED THE storm pass from under a large pine tree low on the mountain. Next to him,

Travis Frank wrung out his hat. "This has to be one of your worst ideas ever, T.D."

"Quit complaining," Wyatt said as he looked around the sodden camp. "It isn't like that was your first thunderstorm—or your last if you're lucky." Travis grumbled under his breath as T.D. emerged from the tree he'd been under, stretched and walked over to them.

"One hell of a storm," the cowboy said, laughing. He'd clearly used the time trapped under the tree while waiting for the hail to stop to take a nip or two from one of the bottles of whiskey he'd brought along.

"You realize that he's going to get us killed or thrown in jail," Travis said under his breath to Wyatt.

"Ready to ride?" T.D. asked jovially. The man had never made it a secret that he loved storms. T.D. loved loud and boisterous, disorder and confusion. He loved chaotic frenzy—and often caused it. It was no wonder the cowboy would enjoy a storm like the one that had just moved through, Wyatt thought as he and Travis left the shelter of the tree.

"What now?" Wyatt asked, clearly not enjoying this. Like him, Travis had noticed that T.D. had been hitting the bottle. His face was flushed, his eyes bright. Sober, T.D. was trying. Drunk, he was hell on wheels.

"Now we catch up to the herd and let the fun begin," T.D. said, grinning. He looked excited, anxious to do whatever he could to cause trouble. Wyatt knew that Jinx would be expecting nothing less. He wondered if T.D. realized that or if he thought he was really going to surprise her when he showed up.

Wyatt hated to think what mayhem T.D. was planning. More than likely the man was playing it by ear, which was even more frightening. He hated to think how drunk T.D. might be by the time they reached Jinx and the herd.

He went to the large pine where he'd tied his horse, swung up into the damp saddle and looked to the towering pine-covered mountain ahead of them. How long before they caught up to the herd? Like T.D., he was anxious. He'd brought his hunting rifle with the scope. Patty's favor rode with him, like a secret tucked in his jacket pocket. A secret that warmed him all through the storm and chilled him the closer they got to catching up to Jinx.

AFTER THE STORM PASSED, the sun had shone bright. They moved the cattle farther up the trail, making better time than Angus had expected. With the storm over, there was a more relaxed feeling in camp that evening when they finally stopped.

They'd reached some more of the old corrals along the trail to summer range.

He'd gone out and killed two blue grouse. Though out of season, he didn't think anyone was going to turn him in after Max fried up the birds until they were crisp on the outside and juicy in the middle. Max had made gravy out of what was left of the cracklings in the huge cast-iron skillet and served it with a large batch of homemade biscuits. Nothing went to waste.

"We're sure as the devil eating better than I expected," Cash said and stuffed half a biscuit into his mouth. "You know what I mean," he said as he swallowed the mouthful. "After the bear got into our grub."

Angus saw Jinx and Max share a look. He had a pretty good idea what it was about. Max had been so sure that he secured the box with the metal meat cooler in it. When Angus had a chance, he'd gotten a good look at the box. He knew that bears were much smarter than most people thought.

He'd once had a cooler stolen off his cabin porch at the ranch by a grizzly bear. That bear did everything possible to get into that old rounded-edge metal cooler, much like the one in the chuck-wagon. When Angus had found it, the grizzly had scratched and clawed and even rolled the cooler down a hillside, but still hadn't been able to get inside it.

There was only one way the black bear had gotten into the one in the chuckwagon. Someone had propped it open like a calling card for any bear in the area. Max was lucky he hadn't awakened to the noise to find a grizzly staring out of the wagon at him.

"Excellent meal," Brick said and everyone around the campfire agreed. This high in the mountains, the temperature began to drop even though it was early June.

After everyone had finished, Royce pulled out a well-used pack of cards and challenged anyone who wanted to play with a poker game. Angus passed, but Brick and Cash said they were in. Ella announced that she would watch and make sure no one cheated.

Jinx got up and walked with Angus to the chuckwagon where Max was seated, watching all of them after cleaning up the dishes. As they approached, the older man rose from where he'd been lounging and announced he was calling it a night.

"I'm sleeping in the woods tonight," Max said. "No more sleeping under the chuckwagon." With that he took his sleeping bag and disappeared into the darkness beyond the campfire.

"Max isn't wild about bears," Jinx whispered with a laugh.

"Hope he doesn't run across one then out in the woods." They both chuckled as she and Angus sat on a log with their backs to the chuckwagon.

"With his luck, Max will run across one on its way to the chuckwagon," she said.

They grew quiet as the campfire popped and the card game grew louder. "I think that's the second time I've heard Royce speak," Jinx said. "You think he deals off the bottom of the deck?"

"I think you can count on it," Angus said with a laugh.

"Your brother—"

"Can take care of himself. Anyway, Ella is looking after him." He smiled to himself, thinking about the three of them working their way across the west from ranch to ranch, camp to camp. It wasn't Brick's first card game. Nor the first one that Ella had watched to make sure he wasn't cheated.

"I'm going to miss this," he said, surprising Jinx—and himself—that he'd spoken his thoughts out loud.

"Are you quitting wrangling?" she asked, turning to him. Her brown eyes had darkened with concern.

"I'll never quit ranching. My parents are counting on me coming back and pretty much taking over running Cardwell Ranch. It's what I was born to do." He smiled and shook his head. "I'm looking forward to it. But I will miss this. Who knows what Brick is going to do. He wants nothing to do with running the ranch."

"You two look so much alike and yet you're so different." He could feel her gaze on him. "What about Ella? What are her plans?"

Angus glanced toward the campfire. Ella's pretty face was lit by the golden firelight. "I don't know. She's welcome to help with the ranch. She's family. But you know how that goes. She could meet some man in a three-piece suit and follow him to the big city."

Jinx laughed. "Can't see that happening, but like you said, you never know. The big city definitely isn't for me. Then again, I have no idea what my future holds."

At the poker game, sparks rose up from the campfire to burn out in the velvet starlit sky overhead. Angus stretched out his long legs, content after a good day in the saddle and a good meal. It didn't hurt that he was sitting here with a beautiful woman, one who intrigued him and always had.

Jinx seemed as relaxed as he felt. He told himself not to get any ideas. The woman needed him. He was a hired man. Once the cattle were at summer pasture, his job would be over.

Still, as he breathed in the night scents that floated around him, he was aware of Jinx next to him in a way he hadn't been aware of a woman in a very long time. The night air felt heavy and seemed too busy with that feeling that anything could happen. He wondered if Jinx felt it or if it was all his imagination.

The thought made him smile. Whatever it was he felt right now, he knew that this was where he belonged at this moment in time. Fate had brought him here. Brought him to this woman whom he'd never forgotten.

"You almost look as if you're enjoying this," Jinx said as she also stretched out her legs to get more comfortable.

He chuckled. He loved nothing better than being in the mountains, listening to the lowing of the cattle and feeling tired after a day in the saddle. But there was also something about Jinx that drew him to her and it was more than a chance meeting all those years ago. It was also more than his being protective.

"I guess it shows, how much I enjoy this," he said, looking over at her. Her brown eyes shone in the ambient firelight; her hair seemed to catch fire, reminding him of how red it was when she was but a girl.

"It does show," she said. "This life gets into your blood. It would be hard to give up."

"I don't plan to. What about you?"

She seemed to be watching the flames of the nearby campfire, the light playing on her face. "After my mother died, my father lost interest in the ranch," Jinx said. "He lost interest in life and went downhill fast. I buried him earlier this spring. I've been running the ranch alone since then. T.D. was supposed to help take up the slack." She looked away. "But I realized right away that all he wanted to do was sell the ranch and live off the profits."

"I'm sorry," Angus said as he focused his gaze on where Brick tossed another log on the fire. A shower of sparks rose up in a flurry of bright red to disappear into the sky overhead.

"This ranch has been in my family for only two generations," she said. "Around here that doesn't mean anything. Most of these people are at least fifth generation ranchers."

"That doesn't mean you aren't wedded to the life and the land. It's hard to let go of something you love. Or someone," he added, remembering what his brother had said.

She smiled over at him. "I let go of T.D. months ago. Unfortunately, getting rid of him isn't as easy as I'd hoped. I filed for divorce but he's contested it, determined to force me to sell and settle with him." Jinx shook her head. "We've only been together less than two years and yet that's enough, according to my lawyer, that T.D. can force me into a settlement. I can't believe what a fool I was."

Angus chuckled. "We've all been there, trust me." Only the crackle of the fire and the occasional burst of laughter or curse broke the stillness around them. He wasn't surprised that in a few minutes, Jinx changed the subject.

"I can't believe my good luck, getting three good hands from Cardwell Ranch," she said, lightening the mood. "Your cousin Ella is just as good as she says she is."

He smiled. "Yep, she can ride circles around me and Brick."

Jinx glanced over at him, the firelight dancing in her eyes. "The two of you let her."

Angus grinned. "Maybe a little, but don't underestimate my cousin. She's special, that one."

"I love how close you three are. Do you have other siblings?"

"An older sister, Mary, and older brother, Hank. And lots more cousins."

"I always wanted a large family."

He studied her in the firelight. "Maybe you'll have one of your own someday." She looked skeptical. "Just because you climbed onto a rank horse once, doesn't mean you quit riding."

She laughed at his analogy. "Rank horse covers T.D. well. I know there are good horses out there as well as men. I'll be much more discerning next time. If there is a next time."

"There will be," he said and met her gaze. He held it, wishing he could take away the hurt he saw in those eyes.

"Your father is a marshal, right?" He nodded. "Your family must miss you."

He smiled, thinking of his mother. "If my mother had her way, we'd all live in the main house and would park our boots under her dining room table every night for dinner."

Jinx nodded. "I've heard about Dana Cardwell Savage. Our mothers were friends, both involved in the cattlewomen's organizations, but I'm sure you already know that. What about Ella's parents?"

"Just her mom, Stacy. She's always taken care of all of us and helped Mom running the house rather than the ranch. She lives on the ranch in one of the cabins up on the side of the mountain." He could feel Jinx's curious gaze on him.

"I'm sure your mother can't wait to have your boots back under her table."

"There's no hurry," he said, chuckling at the truth in her words. "My family, especially my mother and uncle Jordan, have everything under control. My sister takes care of the books for the ranch. They don't need me yet."

"But when they do?"

"I reckon I'll head on home."

Jinx stared up at the swaying pines overhead for a moment. "When my father got sick, I promised myself that I would keep the ranch or die trying."

"Is that what he wanted you to do?"

She seemed surprised by the question. "No, actually, on his deathbed, he made me promise two things. Get rid of T.D. and then the ranch. He thought it would be too much for me and that I would kill myself trying to hang on to it. I guess it's no wonder so many ranchers are selling out to those large companies that move cattle with helicopters and are owned by even larger corporations."

"Ranching isn't an easy way to make a living, that's for sure," Angus agreed. "So your father gave you good advice."

She chuckled. "You mean by kicking T.D. out?" She shook her head, looking rueful. "I'd kicked him out of my bed a long time before that. I should have kicked him off the ranch sooner. But I think I just hated to admit what a mistake I'd made."

"What about selling the ranch?"

Jinx stared again at the campfire for so long, he didn't think she was going to reply. "That's the hard part. I'm not sure I can do it." She let out a bitter bark of a laugh. "But I'm not sure I can keep it, either. T.D. is forcing my hand. I think I'm going to have to sell it just to settle up with him."

"I'm sorry it's come to that."

"My own fault. And maybe my father was right and it's for the best. Just doesn't feel that way right now. Admittedly, T.D.'s got me digging in my heels just out of orneriness." She sighed and seemed glad to see the poker game break up. Angus noted that neither Cash nor Royce looked happy as they headed off to bed. Brick, however, was grinning and joking with Ella, which told him that she'd kept the game honest. That was his cousin. Now his brother had the two men's money in his pocket and had probably made enemies in the process.

"It's going to be another early morning tomorrow," Jinx said but didn't move. "I heard that a male grizzly was seen in this area recently. I thought I'd put Royce and Brick on first watch. Brick's already volunteered."

Angus just bet he had. "I can relieve Brick."

She nodded. "I'll let them know." Like him, she must have hated to leave this quiet spot. There was an intimacy to it. When she looked over at him, their gazes locked for a few long moments.

Jinx pulled her gaze away first and rose to her feet. "I best get some shut-eye," she said. "It was nice visiting with you."

"You, too. Sleep well," he said as he watched

her stop by the campfire to speak with Brick and Ella. Jinx was chuckling to herself as she went to find Royce and Cash before heading to her sleeping bag spread out in the dried pine needles some distance from the fire.

Angus watched her go, telling himself that there was nothing he could do to help Jinx other than to get her cattle to the high country. But even as he thought it, he knew that wouldn't be the end of her problems. And they hadn't gotten the cattle to the high country yet, he reminded himself as he made his way to his own sleeping bag.

All they needed was another long day of moving the herd and then a short one without any more trouble than they'd had and the cattle would be on summer range. Then it would be just a matter of returning to the valley. The job would be over.

As he walked through the darkness of the pines toward where he'd dropped his sleeping bag earlier, he saw Royce ride off with Brick and then part company as they split up to take the first night shift.

He looked around but didn't see Cash. The two worried him, especially after the incident with the bear in the chuckwagon. Since then, though, nothing had happened. So maybe Max had gotten forgetful and left the box holding the meat locker unlocked and cracked open just enough that a bear caught wind of it.

He told himself that in another day and a half they would have completed the job they were hired on to do. He and Ella and Brick could head back to Montana. They would have accomplished what they'd come here for.

Unless Jinx's almost-ex had other plans for them before then.

ELLA COULDN'T SLEEP. She felt restless, even as tired as she was. For a while, she lay staring up into the darkness. Clouds from the aftermath of the storm hung low over the mountainside, blocking out the stars like a thick, dark cloak.

Finally, she rose and walked away from the camp, feeling as if she couldn't breathe. She wasn't sure what was causing it. Earlier she'd tried to reach her mother. But she couldn't get cell phone coverage.

From as far back as she could remember, she'd "sensed" things. She'd been uneasy when they'd stopped by Cardwell Ranch before heading down here to Wyoming. Her mother had been acting strangely. It wasn't anything she could put her finger on. Just a sense that something was wrong.

That feeling had only gotten stronger. Her instincts told her she should saddle up and go home. But she'd signed on to this job and she would stick it out. Especially after meeting Jinx. She wasn't about to leave the woman shorthanded. In a few days they would be headed home. She just hoped that would be soon enough, as she reached the horse corral.

With the clouds hanging so low over the mountainside, she could only make out dark shapes behind the corral fence. She leaned against the railing, breathing in the cold night air, and tried to still her growing unease. She and her mother had always been close since from the beginning it was just the two of them—and of course the rest of the Cardwell/Savage family. As to her father, she knew little about him, only that he'd never been in the picture.

Not that she hadn't had an amazing childhood growing up on Cardwell Ranch. Her mother had seemed happy there after having split with her family years before over what would be done with the ranch following Mary Cardwell's death. Ella knew only a little about the argument that had caused the siblings to fight over the ranch. Apparently, Dana had refused to sell it, while Ella's mother, Stacy, and her uncle Jordan wanted the cash from the sale.

When their mother's will was finally found, it settled the squabble, but by then the damage had been done. It had taken time for Stacy and Jordan to come back to the ranch. Stacy had come back after she had Ella.

She felt fatigue pull at her and started to push off the corral fence when she heard a sound that made her freeze. Someone was moving through the darkness in her direction. Instantly, she was on alert, aware that whoever was moving toward her was moving cautiously, as if not wanting to be heard.

Whoever it was hadn't seen her. She stayed still as the figure grew larger and larger. She knew it wasn't an animal because an animal would have picked up her scent by now.

The shape grew larger and larger until the man was almost on top of her. She watched him look around in the darkness as if to make sure that no one had seen him. She could tell he was listening because the night was dark; he couldn't see any farther than she could.

Then, as if believing he was alone, he reached for the latch on the corral holding the horses.

"Cash?"

He jumped and then froze for a moment before he slowly let go of the latch. Turning just as slowly, he squinted into the darkness. He took a few steps in her direction. "Oh, it's you. I didn't see you standing there." He sounded winded as if she'd scared him. Or worse, she'd caught him.

"What's going on?" she asked, even though she had a pretty good idea.

"Nothing," he said as he moved closer. "Just checking on the horses."

"Looked like you were going to open the gate and let all the horses out."

He let out a nervous laugh as he closed the distance between them. "Why would I do that?"

"I was wondering the same thing." He was close now, so close she could see the dark holes of his eyes.

He glanced around and then said quietly, "I thought everyone was asleep."

"I figured you did."

His gaze settled on her. His lips curled into a smirk. "What's a woman like you doing up here on this mountain with a bunch of men anyway?"

"You have a problem with it?"

"Me?" He leaned toward her. "Naw, but some men would think a young, good-looking woman riding with a group of males was just asking for it."

His words sent a chill through her, but she didn't let it show. Except for the fact that she'd eased her hand down to the holstered gun at her hip. "Men like that end up dead. Good thing you're not one of them. Otherwise, I'd advise you to sleep with one eye open."

He cleared his throat as his gaze dropped to her hand resting on the butt of her pistol. "That sounds like a threat."

"Only to men who don't respect women."

Ella heard a soft chuckle from the darkness before Jinx materialized out from behind Cash.

"There a problem here?" the trail boss asked, startling the already nervous Cash.

He spun around. "Not from me," Cash said quickly and took a few steps away from Ella.

When Jinx shifted her gaze to her in question, Ella simply shook her head and said, "I believe Cash was just on his way to bed. He's thinking about sleeping with one eye open."

He shot her a mean look before checking his expression and turning to Jinx. "In case either of you care, I'm a light sleeper." He touched the gun at his hip.

"Sleep well," Jinx said.

As Cash headed toward camp, Ella heard him mumble something about women not knowing their place.

Jinx sighed as she watched him disappear into the darkness before she turned back to Ella. "Now, what was really going on out here?"

"I couldn't sleep. Cash didn't see me out here in the dark. I think he was planning to release the horses. He was starting to open the gate when I spoke up. He said he was just checking his horse."

"But you don't believe him." Jinx nodded. "Best get some sleep."

Chapter Seven

Wide awake now, Jinx saddled up her horse. Royce had offered to take the first watch, along with Brick. So far it had been quiet. Other than the black bear that had gotten into their larder, they hadn't seen any more bears.

But with the grizzlies out of hibernation and hungry, they were a threat to the herd. She'd seen how easily one could take down beef on the hoof. She and the others had to be cautious, especially of the ones with cubs, she thought as she rode out toward the south end of the herd.

But the wild animals weren't the only threat. She thought about what Ella had told her, trusting the woman's instincts along with her own. Cash needed to go. But maybe after being caught, he wouldn't be a problem. Jinx sighed. She needed him just a little longer. If he'd hired on to cause her trouble, then maybe he was already working with T.D. Otherwise, there was a good chance he would turn on her once her almost-ex did show up. It was only a matter of time before that happened. T.D. was too predictable not to follow her up here.

Pushing thoughts of him away, she considered what to do about Cash. As the last of the clouds passed, the night sky was suddenly ablaze with stars and a sliver of moon. Nothing seemed to move in the dark stillness as she rode south along the edge of the herd.

On nights like this, she couldn't help but think of her father. She missed him so much it took her breath away. He'd been everything to her since she was a girl. He'd always been there when she needed him. When her mother had died, he'd comforted her more than she could him. He would have known what to do about Royce and Cash.

Just as he'd known that T.D. was all wrong for her. He'd tried to talk her out of marrying the cowboy, but she'd been in love.

Love. She could laugh now at how starry-eyed she'd been. T.D. had definitely charmed her. He'd made her feel beautiful. Her feelings for the few boyfriends she'd had seemed silly in comparison. T.D. had been her first honest-to-goodness love affair. He took her to fancy restaurants in Jackson Hole, getting her out of her jeans and boots, making her feel like a desirable woman.

That thought made her heart ache. She'd felt

like a princess with T.D. Why wouldn't she marry him? He'd said and done all the right things.

"I know you want your father to walk you down the aisle," T.D. had said one night. "I want that for you. That's why I don't think we should put off getting married."

She'd been dragging her feet. There'd been little red flags. T.D.'s credit card not working. Times when he'd forgotten his wallet. She'd been happy to pay. Another time there'd been the man whom T.D. had purposely avoided at the rodeo, saying the man was a poor sport at cards. Later, she would learn about his gambling habits. But back then, there'd been enough that she'd been wary of when it came to marrying T.D. He had talked a good line, but she questioned how much help he would be on the ranch.

But then her father had gotten sick. T.D. had been right. She'd dreamed of her father walking her down the aisle. They'd decided to get married, rushing into it even as her father was telling her to wait and be sure this was the man for her.

An owl hooted down at her from a tree limb, startling her out of her thoughts. She reined in her horse, realizing that she still hadn't seen Royce. He was supposed to be riding herd tonight along with Brick. She could hear Brick to the north playing his harmonica, but there was no sign of Royce.

A horse whinnied from the darkness. She

spurred hers forward, following the sound to find Royce's horse tied to a tree. Quietly, she slid off her mount and approached the man on the ground, gun drawn, only to find him sound asleep under the large pine.

Walking up to him, she kicked the worn sole of his boot. He shot up, fumbling for his gun as he blinked wildly and tried to wake up.

"Sorry," he said, scrambling to his feet. "Mother Nature called. I got off my horse and sat down for a minute. Guess I fell asleep."

"Guess so," she said. "Go on back to camp. I'll take it from here."

Royce picked up his Stetson from the dried pine needles and, head down, untied his horse. He hesitated for a moment as if he wanted to say something more in his defense. But apparently, he changed his mind, swung up on his horse and left.

Jinx watched him go, figuring she knew why Huck Chambers had let the two go. If just being lazy was all she had to worry about, she could live with that a few more days. But she feared there was more when it came to those two, especially after Ella's earlier suspicions about Cash.

Angus woke shortly before he saw Jinx ride out. He rolled out and headed for his horse, figuring he'd relieve his brother so Brick could get some sleep. It didn't take much to find him at the front of the herd. Angus simply followed the sound of Brick's harmonica. His brother always carried the musical instrument in his hip pocket, seemingly lost without it.

As he approached, his brother kept playing an old Western song that their grandfather Angus had taught him. He and Brick had been named after their grandfathers. Angus Cardwell played in a band with his brother Harlan, while Brick Savage had been a marshal, like their father.

Brick finished the tune, holding the last note until Angus rode up alongside him. "We've got company," his brother said quietly. His first thought was a grizzly. "Three of them. I spotted their fire. It's almost as if they want us to know they're down there."

"T.D.," Angus said. He'd been expecting him before this. Three riders on horses could easily catch a slow-moving herd. The question now was what happened next.

"What do you think his plan is?" Brick asked.

T.D. didn't seem like a man who would have a plan. Instead, he bet the cowboy made decisions on the spur of the moment. It was another reason, Angus knew, that the man was dangerous. He'd learned from his marshal father that one of the most volatile situations involved a domestic dispute. And now he and his brother and cousin were right in the middle of Jinx and T.D.'s.

"I would imagine he plans to surprise us," Angus said.

"You sure we shouldn't go down there and surprise them?"

He shook his head. "Short of shooting them, all we would do is play into T.D.'s hands. He wants to torment Jinx. Better to ignore them as long as we can. Otherwise, I'm afraid there might be bloodshed."

His brother nodded, but looked disappointed. Brick wasn't one to back down from a fight. He'd gotten his namesake's temper and his other grandfather's musical talent, while Angus had taken more after their father. Hudson Savage was easygoing, solid as granite and just as dependable. He thought before he spoke and it took a lot to rile him.

"Get some sleep," Angus told his twin. "Jinx said we're moving out early again."

He saw his brother glance down the mountain to where the men were camped.

"Let's not say anything to Jinx," Angus said. "Not yet. No reason to worry her when so far, T.D. and his friends haven't done anything."

"Not yet," Brick said as he pocketed his harmonica and rode back toward camp.

T.D. TOOK A DRINK from the pint of whiskey he'd brought and stared into the flames of the campfire. He felt antsy but he knew that Wyatt was right. They'd had a long day on the trail, pushing hard once they finally hit their saddles at almost midday. They'd caught up to Jinx and the herd before sundown.

Wyatt had insisted that it wouldn't be smart to do anything until they'd rested their horses and come up with a plan. *Wyatt and his plans*, he thought with a silent curse as he raised his gaze from the fire to consider his friends.

"You really hit the bottom of the barrel with these two, didn't you, Junior?" his father had said when he'd begun running with Wyatt and Travis at a young age. "But then I guess it isn't easy to find two dumb enough to tag along with you given where you're headed."

He thought of his father's smirk, his words harder than a backhand and more hurtful. Tucker David Sharp Senior had never given him any credit. The man had been convinced early on that his namesake wasn't going to amount to anything and neither were his friends.

Well, all that was about to change. At least for him. Once he got the ranch…

The more he'd thought about it, the more he wanted the whole thing. Half would force Jinx to sell her precious ranch, which should have been satisfaction enough, he supposed. And it would put a good chunk of change into his pocket—temporarily. Once he paid off his gambling debts, he wouldn't have all that much left. Also, he knew himself well enough to know that money burned a hole in his pocket. He'd gamble, trying to use the money to make more money and probably lose it all.

But if he had the whole ranch, then he could show his father that he'd been wrong about him. Too bad the senior Sharp was in his grave, but he could watch from his special place in hell. *Look at me now, Dad. See how wrong you were?*

He would rename the ranch after himself and make it the best damned ranch in the valley. He took another sip of the whiskey. Or maybe he'd just sell it and live off the money. Maybe he'd have to sell it to pay his gambling debts. If he couldn't borrow against it. He imagined walking into the bank and asking for a loan against his ranch. *His* ranch. He liked the sound of that.

"You might want to go easy on that stuff," Travis said from across the fire as he watched him take another slug from the whiskey bottle. T.D. shot him a dark look. "Just sayin' I agree with Wyatt. We should have a plan so we don't get our fool selves shot. Jinx ain't alone up there."

"Don't you think I know that?" T.D. snapped. He thought of the cowhand who'd come to his wife's rescue the other night at the ranch. He'd seen the others, as well. A motley bunch if there ever was one. He'd recognized two of them, Royce Richards and Cash Andrews, both worthless as the day was long. Working for Jinx was probably the only job they could get after Huck had booted them off his place.

But dumb and worthless aside, they'd all be armed. And Jinx was no fool. She'd know he'd be coming after her—if she didn't already. He got up to throw another tree limb onto the fire. He couldn't wait until tomorrow. When he got the ranch he was going to buy himself a brand-new pickup, the best money could buy. He'd show them. He'd show them all. T. D. Sharp was somebody.

Chapter Eight

The next morning Jinx pulled Royce aside. "Here's your pay," she said, handing him the money she'd brought along, already anticipating that Royce and Cash wouldn't last more than a day or so. "I think it's best if we part company now rather than later."

"You have to be kidding me. Just because I fell asleep?" Royce said incredulously. "I suppose you've never done that while on watch?"

"No, I haven't, and I've been doing this since I was six."

He shook his head. "I guess we all can't be as perfect as you, Ms. Trail Boss. By the way, how'd you get the nickname Jinx anyway?"

"It was just something my father called me, if you must know."

"Oh, I thought it was because you brought bad luck to everyone around you," Royce said, his eyes narrowing angrily. "Seems all those things T.D.'s been saying about you are true."

She didn't bother to comment as she turned. Over her shoulder, she said, "You're welcome to have breakfast before you pack up and leave."

"No, thanks," he said to her back. "I've had enough. At least now I understand what your husband had to put up with."

Jinx kept walking. It was hard not to take the bait. Royce had a lot in common with T.D. Both blamed other people for how their lives had turned out. They really seemed to think that if their luck changed, everything would come up roses. They preferred to blame luck rather than their lack of hard work.

As she was headed down the side of the mountain to where the chuckwagon sat, she saw Max and knew, even before she heard him carrying on, that something else had happened.

By the time she reached him, Angus and Brick had joined him. Angus was squatting on the ground in front of one of the wagon's wheels.

"What's wrong?" she asked as she moved closer.

"Someone sabotaged the wagon," Brick told her.

"Don't worry. Angus thinks he can fix it," Max said, disbelief in his tone. "Then again, he thinks he can make eatable biscuits."

She caught Angus's amused grin. "I'm going to have to make my biscuits before this cattle drive is over just to show Max," he said to Jinx.

"If you must," she said, unable not to smile.

"My honor is at stake," he said as they all stood around the wagon wheel in question.

"So you think you can fix the wheel?" she asked.

"A couple of spokes were pried loose," Angus said. "Brick and I can knock them back into place. They should hold enough that we can get the wagon off the mountain. You can get it fixed once we get back to civilization, though."

"Civilization? You do know this is Wyoming, right?" she joked, then sobered. "So this was done purposely?"

Angus nodded. "There's something else you should know." He hesitated as he saw Cash headed their way. "T.D. and his friends have caught up to us."

"You think they did this?" she asked.

He shook his head. "It was someone in camp."

She let out an angry breath. Turning, she saw Royce riding off. Did he do this?

Cash joined them. "What's going on?"

JINX CONSIDERED CASH, wondering if she shouldn't send him down the mountain with his pay, as well. But she figured Royce had done this after her encounter with him last night. "My ex-husband and a couple of his friends have followed us. It could be a problem."

"Looks like it already is a problem," Cash said, eyeing the wheel on the wagon.

"We aren't sure who did that," Angus said as Royce disappeared over a rise.

Cash followed his gaze. "So you paid off Royce?"

"I did," Jinx said, half expecting Cash to quit and go with his buddy. "I'm saying it could get dangerous. I know you didn't sign on for that."

He nodded his head in agreement before shrugging. "I hate to ask what's for breakfast," he said, as if losing interest in the conversation.

"Ella caught more fish and I know there are biscuits," Brick told him.

"That'll do," Cash said and started toward the fire Max had already laid that morning. "It's just another day and a half, right?" he asked over his shoulder.

"Right," she said to his retreating backside before looking at Angus. He shook his head as if to say it was her decision whether or not to keep him on.

The news about T.D. hadn't come as a surprise. She'd known he couldn't leave well enough alone. It gave her whiplash the way one moment he was begging for her to take him back and the next threatening to sue for half the ranch. More and more, she just wanted it over.

"Should have killed T.D. when I had the chance," Max mumbled under his breath.

"And what would I do without you while you went to prison?" she demanded.

"Starve," he said flatly.

"Exactly." She coaxed a smile out of him as he dished up her breakfast and she went to sit near the campfire. Cash got up without a word to go stand in line for his breakfast. She told herself it was just another full day and night. They would reach summer pasture with the herd by noon tomorrow and then head off the mountain.

Not that it would be over for her, but at least she didn't have to worry about her wranglers and Max up here in the mountains with T.D. and his friends. She felt anxious, though, knowing that he was so nearby. She would double the patrol tonight. Knowing T.D., he just might decide to strike once he was drunk enough.

"You're awfully quiet," Angus said as he sat down next to his cousin after getting his breakfast plate. Everyone else had eaten while Angus and Brick had worked on the wagon wheel. They would be moving out soon.

"It hit me that this is probably the last time that we'll do this together, the three of us," Ella said.

"Why would you say that?" he asked, surprised.

She shot him a don't-con-a-conman look. "Because it's time. I've suspected you've known it for a while." Her gaze left him to find Brick. "I'm worried how your brother is going to take it. But I'm sure he'll fall in love, get married, have a passel of kids and be just fine."

Angus shook his head. He couldn't see it. Brick loved women. Loved the chase. But once he caught one, he was already looking for his next challenge. He studied his cousin for a moment. It would take a very special woman for him to ever settle down.

"What about you?" he asked. Ella looked surprised. "There a cowboy out there for you?"

"A cowboy?" She chuckled. "I'm thinking more like a banker or a stockbroker, someone who wears a three-piece suit to work. What are you smiling about?"

"You. I know you, cuz."

"Maybe I'm tired of cowboys and want something different."

"Maybe a man who drives a car that has to be plugged in."

"Nothing wrong with saving the planet."

Angus scoffed. "Seriously, what would you do with a man who didn't know how to drive a stick shift or back up a trailer or ride a horse?"

"Anything I wanted," she said with a laugh.

He shook his head. "Well, I hope you find him, but it's not going to be on this mountain."

"I know." She met his gaze. "So you're saying

it's time we grew up and settled down. I guess this is the last time for the three of us to be wrangling together."

"It makes me sad to think about it," Angus said and took a bite of his breakfast. He didn't have much of an appetite after seeing what someone had done to the chuckwagon wheel. Talking about this wasn't helping. "We've had some good times. I wouldn't take anything for the years we've been on the road."

Ella nodded. "What will you do?"

"Go home. The ranch needs some young blood." He studied her out of the corner of his eye as he ate. "I know your mother wishes you would stay on the ranch. You know there is a place for you in the business."

"I know. I don't know what I'll do. But I'm not worried. It will come to me."

He shook his head. "You amaze me. You have so much faith in how things will work out. Don't you ever worry?"

"Of course I worry. But I do think a lot of it is out of my hands."

"Stacy will be disappointed if you don't stay on the ranch."

Ella smiled. "My mother can handle disappointment. She's had plenty of it in her life. Anyway, she's told me repeatedly that she just wants me to be happy."

He laughed. "My mother told me the same thing."

"You don't think she means it?"

"She does. And she doesn't." He shook his head. "Dana has her heart set on me coming back to the place. Fortunately, I'm a born rancher. It's what I want to do, always have."

"You're thinking of Brick."

Angus nodded. "He doesn't want to ranch. But he doesn't know what he wants."

"I predict that one day he'll meet a woman and everything will be clear to him. But that doesn't mean it will be easy."

"You see that in the campfire flames?" he joked.

"Pretty much." She met his gaze, smiling. "Same thing is going to happen to you. If it hasn't already."

Angus finished his breakfast and rose, laughing. "I trust your instincts, cuz, but a woman isn't always the answer and from what I've seen, love is never easy."

Ella merely nodded. But as he walked away, he heard her say, "We'll see."

THROUGH THE MORNING mist hanging in the pines, T.D. saw Royce coming and picked up his rifle where he'd leaned it against a tree. He ratcheted live ammo into the chamber as the man rode toward him. "That's far enough," he said, raising the weapon.

"Take it easy," Royce said and reined in to lift his hands in surrender.

"What do you want?"

"I just got fired by your wife. What do you think I want? A kind word, a soft bed, a decent meal?" he said sarcastically. "I want to get even with her. Then I want the other stuff along with a stiff drink or two. I heard you were offering a...reward of sorts for anyone who...didn't help your wife." Royce chuckled. "I've done my part."

"By hiring on to help her get her cattle to summer range?" T.D. demanded.

"Maybe I made it more difficult for her. They're probably trying to figure out how to fix one of the wagon wheels right now."

T.D. smiled. "Why don't you swing down out of that saddle and we can talk about it? I do have a little whiskey."

"I just thought you might," Royce said as he dismounted and tied his horse to the closest tree limb.

Resting his rifle against the tree again, T.D. dug in their supplies for another pint of whiskey. "Have a sip and then tell me what's going on in the other camp."

Royce took the bottle, unscrewed the lid and gulped.

T.D. snatched it from him. "I said a sip." He wiped the top off with his hand and took a drink.

"Where are the others?" Royce asked, looking around.

"Doing some surveillance work. How many men does Jinx have?"

The cowboy pulled up a log next to the fire. "Four at the moment, not counting the old cook and the woman she hired on."

"I thought I saw a cowgirl by the bunkhouse the other night." He laughed. "She's that hard up, is she, that she had to hire a woman?"

"The woman's good. Definitely wouldn't underestimate her," Royce said.

"That's it?"

"Cash Andrews is up there. At least for the moment. She's only got another day and a half and she'll have the cattle to the high country. Cash will do what he can to make it harder for her." Royce smiled. "He was going to let the horses out but that...cowgirl, as you called her, caught him."

T.D. shook his head. "Sometimes it feels as if women will take over the world unless we do something about it."

"I'd take another drink. The trail boss didn't allow liquor."

He laughed, knowing all about Jinx's rules. He'd played hell living by them. He handed the whiskey bottle to the man, ready to grab it back.

But this time Royce took a drink and passed it over to him again. "She's already been having some bad luck," he said, grinning as if he knew this was music to T.D.'s ears. "A black bear got into the food. Seems someone left the metal box with the meat and eggs in it open. This morning the chuckwagon wheel had been worked over. Thought you might like to hear that."

"Poor Jinx." He eyed the cowboy. "If you're not in a hurry to get back down to the valley, maybe you'd like to hire on with me."

"You're offering me a job?"

"I'm going to be running the Flying J Bar MC soon," T.D. boasted. "But this job is more about getting even. The wages aren't good, but the satisfaction is guaranteed."

Chapter Nine

The day passed without any trouble, surprising Angus. When Jinx rode over to him late in the afternoon, he mentioned his surprise to her.

"He'll wait until tonight," she said. "He'll wait until he thinks we are all asleep. It could be a long night since I plan to double the patrol tonight. But tomorrow will be an easy day and then it will be over."

It just wouldn't be over for Jinx. Not that Angus thought they would get by that easily. T.D. had ridden a long way. He wasn't going to let them get away without making trouble for Jinx and the herd.

It was dusk by the time they made camp and Max cooked the grouse Angus and Brick had shot. Cash straggled in, limping.

"Stepped in a hole," he said as he plopped down on a log by the fire. "It's killing me." He turned as Jinx walked up and asked what was going on. "I don't think I can ride watch tonight.

I can barely walk. Hurts like hell even in the saddle."

Jinx seemed to study him for a moment. Like him, Angus figured she had been expecting something like this. "You quitting, Cash?"

He shook his head without looking at her. "Just not sure I'll be much help."

She nodded. "I'll settle up with you in the morning. Unless you're thinking of taking off tonight?"

"Mornin' will do," he said, still not looking at her.

All day Angus had seen her watching for T.D. while keeping an eye on Cash. The wrangler had seemed restless. When they'd stopped for lunch, Angus had noticed that Cash barely touched his biscuit sandwich of leftover fried fish from that morning. Normally, the man ate as if he feared it would be his last meal.

"I'll be glad to have Cash gone," Jinx said later as she and Angus rode out to take first watch. "I'm kicking myself for hiring him and Royce."

"You did what you had to do," Angus told her. "Anyway, they haven't caused that much trouble."

"There is still tonight," she said as she looked down the mountainside.

He'd seen the campfire below them. He'd also seen four men standing around it. Royce had joined ranks with T.D. and his friends. *No big surprise there*, he thought. That just left the question of Cash. He made Angus nervous, like he did Jinx.

To make matters worse, the night was dark, the clouds low. A breeze in the pines made the boughs moan woefully. It was the kind of night that you wouldn't see someone sneaking up on you until it was too late. Worse, they'd had to leave Cash in camp alone except for Max. Brick and Ella were on patrol on the other side of the herd.

Angus felt anxious and he knew that was what was really bothering Jinx. Knowing T.D. was out there and not alone… "Cash'll be gone in the morning."

She nodded, but still looked worried as they rode slowly around the northern perimeter of the herd. "What if Royce hooks up with T.D.?"

He hated to tell her. "He already has, I'm pretty sure."

She let out a bark of a laugh. "Cash is bound to join them, as well. They'll outnumber us."

He couldn't argue that. "We'll do what we have to do." He'd been thinking about what they could do if T.D. attacked them. He thought the cowboy would be more sneaky than that. But neither of them knew what the man would do.

"I just don't want to have to kill anyone," she said.

He didn't, either, but what neither of them said but both knew was that they would if they had to.

Jinx considered riding down the mountain and confronting T.D. But they would merely have the same argument. Worse, he'd be with his friends so he'd show off. She couldn't chance making things worse by embarrassing him in front of them. At this point she had no idea how to handle T.D. He'd gone off the rails and she couldn't see this ending any way but badly.

She wondered what he had planned. As if he ever planned anything. Maybe he thought he could intimidate her by simply following her up here. If he'd hoped his presence would rattle her, well, it did. She'd been waiting for the other shoe to drop for some time now. T.D. was nothing if not determined. He wouldn't give up. Now more than ever he had to save face with his buddies and everyone else in the county. Too bad he didn't put that kind of determination into a job.

She thought of T.D.'s father and what little he'd told her about him in a weak moment. The man had sounded horrible, which she knew could explain partially at least why T.D. was the way he was. He saw himself as a victim. Right or wrong, he believed his actions, no matter what they were, were warranted.

Like now, it was clear that he felt he had to do something to make this right when this was the worst thing he could do. But there would be no reasoning with him. The only thing she could control were her own actions. Keep fighting T.D.? Or give in?

Giving in meant putting the ranch up for sale. She couldn't afford to borrow against it, not when she knew that she and Max couldn't run it by themselves.

Before her father died, he'd seen the handwriting on the wall. "I'm getting too old to do this anymore," he'd told her. "Even if T.D. was worth his salt, this place takes more hired hands than we can afford. It's why so many families are selling out. Even the ones with a half dozen sons who could run the place are being sold because younger folk want more out of life than feeding cattle when it is twenty below zero, calving in a blizzard or branding in a dust storm or pouring rain."

"We've done all of that and survived," she'd argued. "I love this life. I'm not ready to give it up."

"It's dying, Jinx. I need you to promise me that when I'm gone, you'll put the place up for sale and move on with your life."

She hadn't been able to do that. "I'll try." That was all she'd said that time and then again later when her father was on his deathbed. He'd known how hard it would be on her to let go of the ranch—especially being forced to by her soon-to-be ex-husband. The property settlement was the only thing holding up her freedom. But if it meant giving up the life she loved, what kind of freedom was that?

She'd already been offered a fair price for her herd—if she got the cattle to summer grazing land. She wouldn't even have to bring them back down in the fall. Also, there were several ranchers around, interested in her place. A local Realtor had come out not long after Jinx's father's death.

"With what you'd make off the ranch, you could do anything you've ever dreamed of," the woman had said.

"What if running this ranch is what I've dreamed of?" Jinx had asked her.

The woman had nodded and given her a pitying look. "Then I guess your dream has come true." She'd handed Jinx her card. "In case your dream changes," she'd said and left.

WYATT SMELLED DINNER cooking and felt his stomach roil.

"You goin' to have one?" Travis asked. T.D. had put him in charge of the food they would need. "Just a couple of days' worth. Keep it simple," T.D. had said foolishly.

"Hot dogs again?" Wyatt asked.

"Hey, T.D. said to keep it simple. I cut you a stick to cook yours on. What more do you want?"

Real food, he wanted to say. Like his mother cooked every night. He picked up the stick with the sharp end Travis had whittled with his pocket-knife and looked around. "Where's T.D.?" Travis shrugged. Digging a hot dog out of the insulated pack, he wondered how long they could survive on hot dogs, cookies and trail mix. Not long since the supply was dwindling fast.

"Maybe he changed his mind." Travis sounded hopeful.

Like him, Wyatt figured Travis was ready to get off this mountain. It was cold at night this time of year and hot during the day. They'd spent hours in the saddle following Jinx and her herd of cattle, only to stop when Jinx did and make camp below the mountain. T.D. had done nothing but drink and complain about his soon-to-be ex-wife. Hopefully, this foolishness would be over soon because they were running out of food and now they had Royce to feed, as well.

Speaking of the devil, the wrangler ambled out of the woods. "I'll take one of those," Royce said of the hot dogs. Travis pointed at the stick he'd made him. "Where's T.D.?"

They both shrugged. Wyatt saw that his hot dog was pretty much black and pulled it out of the fire. Travis tossed him a bun and a plastic squeeze container of mustard.

"You have any ketchup?" Royce asked.

"We're roughin' it," Travis said. "It's mustard or nothing. We didn't know we'd have...company."

Royce laughed at that. "Well, when the fireworks start, you're going to be glad you have my company."

Wyatt shared a look with Travis. What had T.D. told Royce? Fireworks? He didn't like the sound of this.

At the sound of a twig breaking off to their right, they all froze for a moment. Wyatt was going for his gun, thinking the smell of the hot dogs cooking had brought a bear into camp. It wouldn't be the first time.

Fortunately, it was just T.D. He came walking into camp, grinning.

"The fun is about to begin," he announced and looked at Travis. "That one for me?" he said of the hot dog Travis had cooked perfectly.

Travis looked from the hot dog to T.D. and back before he sighed and said, "Why not?"

"Then we'd better pull up camp," T.D. said, taking the hot dog and bun and reaching for the mustard. "We might have to move fast."

Oh, hell, Wyatt thought. What has the cowboy done now?

Chapter Ten

Angus caught a whiff of something on the breeze that froze his blood. *Smoke?* Jinx must have caught the scent, as well. She shot him a look and then the two of them were yelling for the others as they raced toward the smoke rising on the horizon.

Angus hadn't gone far when he saw the flames licking at the grass along the tree line—and in the direction of the herd. He jumped off his horse, pulled off his jacket and began beating the flames back. Next to him, Jinx was doing the same.

As Ella and Brick joined them, they formed a line, pushing the fire back. Had it been fall, they wouldn't have been able to stop the wildfire. But with the new grass mixed in with what was left of the dried fall vegetation, the fire wasn't moving fast.

The four of them worked quickly, beating back the flames. Angus had no doubt who had started the fire. He'd seen firsthand what T. D. Sharp was like that night at the ranch. He'd expected trouble, but not this. The man was a damned fool. Didn't he realize that he could start a forest fire that could spread through the mountains—killing everything, him included?

Every year forest fires burned across this part of the west. They often grew even with the states throwing everything they could at the flames. Most weren't put out until the first snows in the fall. That was Angus's fear now. If this fire spread, it would kill more than Jinx's herd.

At first it appeared that they would never be able to hold the fire off. Then as if granted a miracle, a spring squall came through just before daylight, drenching them and the mountainside with a soaking rain shower. The rain did most of the work, but they still had to finish putting out hot spots.

By then it was midday. But they'd kept the fire away from the herd and they'd put it out. With most of the mountainside wet from the rainstorm that had come through before dawn, T.D. would play hell getting another fire started until everything dried out. By then they would have the cattle in the high country and have returned to the valley.

Angus figured T.D. would lose interest once Jinx was no longer on the mountain. There would be no reason to kill a bunch of cattle, especially when it sounded as if he would get half the ranch in the divorce. So half the cattle would also be his. That was if the man had thought that far ahead.

But first they had to get the herd the rest of the way to summer range. What else did T.D. have planned for them before they all went back down into the valley?

"Here's where it started," Brick called. Jinx walked over to where his brother was pointing at the ground and Angus followed.

He knew what he was going to find even before he reached his twin. Boot tracks in the soft, wet, scorched earth and the charred remains of a bandanna soaked with fuel oil.

"Whoever started the fire had planned this," Jinx said with disgust as she took a whiff of the bandanna. The cowboys wouldn't have had fuel oil on them. They had to have brought it with them. She shook her head, planting her hands on her hips as she looked out across the pasture to where the herd moved restlessly. If Angus hadn't smelled the fire so quickly... If the flames had gotten away from them...

"What now?" She sounded close to tears but quickly cleared her throat. "What's he going to do next?" She looked at Angus, but it was Brick who spoke.

"What if it wasn't your ex?" Brick said as he

looked around. "Anyone seen Cash?" Angus realized he hadn't seen Max, either.

They made their way back to camp. Angus wasn't surprised to see Cash's horse gone. Max was busy finishing making breakfast. "I thought you might all be hungry," he said as he took them in. "Figured I was better here than fighting the fire."

"When did Cash leave?" Jinx asked.

"Soon as he smelled smoke," Max said. "He hightailed it out of here. Said he'd catch up with you at the ranch to get his pay."

Jinx mumbled something under her breath.

"I think we should end this now," Brick said and looked at him. "Let's go pay them a visit."

"No," Jinx said, her gaze on Angus. "We have cattle to move. That's why we rode up here. That's what we're going to do. We've lost some time, but we're going to get these cattle to the high country. But first I'm going to wash some of this soot off. Thank you all for being here." With that she turned on her boot heel and walked away.

"I think we're growing on her," Brick said with a chuckle.

Angus smiled. "That is one determined young woman and she's right. We take care of the herd. That's our job." He felt his twin's gaze on him.

"She likes you," his brother said.

"I'm not trying to—"

"That's just it, Angus. You don't have to try." With that, Brick turned and walked away.

Angus sighed, tired of his brother's need to compete. He doubted it had anything to do with Jinx. Brick just liked to win. Angus was determined, though, that it wasn't going to be a problem between them. After this job was over...well, as Ella said, maybe it was time that the three of them went their own way.

Smelling of smoke and covered with soot, Angus headed for the creek. He needed to cool down anyway. He and Brick weren't that much alike sometimes. He had wanted to go after T.D., too, which told him that Jinx was right about ordering them not to. He'd never been impulsive. Now wasn't the time to start.

And what if some of T.D.'s men hit the herd, scattering it, while he and Brick were off looking for him?

Reaching the creek, he stopped under a large old pine tree and pulled off his boots. Pulling his gun, he pushed it down in one of his boots and then took off his belt and tossed it beside the boots.

He considered stripping down, but realized his clothing could use a wash. Or at least a dip in water. He stepped to the edge of the stream, picking a dark spot where the water ran deep and then in a few strides dove headfirst into the shimmering pool.

He'd known it would be freezing cold. Just as he'd known it would take his breath away. But knowing was one thing; feeling it clear to his bones was another.

He shot up out of the water and let out a yell and then a laugh.

"How's the water?" asked Jinx from the shadow of the large pine.

"Warm," he lied, grinning as he watched her pull off her boots, then her holstered gun, before she did what he had done.

He moved aside to give her plenty of room. She dove in and came up fast, spitting out the icy water as she did. He couldn't help but laugh.

"Cold enough for you?" he asked, still grinning even though he realized he couldn't feel his lower extremities.

"I've felt colder," she said and then laughed as the two of them rushed to the shore, grateful to be out of the snow-fed water.

Angus pulled off his shirt and hung it over a limb to dry in the sun. A warming spring breeze rippled over his bare flesh.

Jinx had sat down on a rock, leaning back to close her eyes. "Maybe your brother is right," she said.

"Brick is seldom right," he joked. "That you

even think he might be proves you've lost your mind."

She smiled and opened her eyes to look at him. "If anything happens to you and the others because of me..."

"We knew what we were getting into."

She studied him on the rock where he'd sat down beside the stream. He'd stretched out his long legs in the hopes that his jeans would dry some in the sun without him having to remove them. "Ella told me. Your mother asked you to come help me?"

"It's what neighbors do."

She laughed at that and she freed her hair from the braid she'd had it in. The wet coppery mass of curls fell around her face, dropping down past her breasts. "We're hardly neighbors."

"We're ranchers. Ranchers help other ranchers."

"Maybe where you live."

"Don't blame the other ranchers. They're in a tough spot."

She met his gaze. "Do you always give everyone the benefit of the doubt?"

"Hardly. But I try," he admitted. "Few people want to get in the middle of a family squabble."

"Is that what this is?" she asked, holding his gaze. "But the three of you did."

He chuckled. "By now you must realize that we lack good sense."

She pulled her gaze away to look toward the stream. "I hate that everyone knows my troubles."

"Don't. We all need help sometimes."

She smiled, shaking her head. "You must be wondering what I saw in T.D. What would make me marry someone like him?"

"That's your business."

"Still, you must think me a fool."

He laughed softly, turning his face up to the sun. "If you'd met my last girlfriend… We all have a mistake in our past that we'd like to forget."

"You're an awfully nice man, Angus Savage."

He could feel the sun warming his chest and hear the quiet babble of the stream. But what really warmed him were her words. Sitting here with her, he felt a contentment that he hadn't felt in a long time.

His eyes opened as he sensed her closeness. She stood over him for a moment, before she sat down next to him and turned until she was facing him only inches part. He held his breath as she reached toward him. His heart thundered in his chest as he felt her cool fingertips trace the scar on his chin.

"I'M CURIOUS," JINX SAID, her voice sounding strange even to her. "How did you get that scar?"

She watched Angus swallow, then seem to relax, his blue eyes bright with humor. "Well, it's kind of an amusing story." He smiled. "I got pushed out of a barn loft when I was eleven."

"That's awful."

He sat up straighter until they were eye to eye. "It was my fault. I asked for it."

"You asked to be pushed out of a barn loft?"

"I was teasing her. She warned me that if I didn't stop she would knock me into tomorrow."

"She?" Jinx felt goose bumps break out over her skin and for a moment she could smell the fresh hay in the barn, feel the breeze on her face, remember that cute cowboy who'd taunted her. Her heart began to pound.

His smile broadened. "She was a spitfire, as fiery as her hair back then."

Jinx felt heat rush to her cheeks. "Tell me her name wasn't JoRay McCallahan."

"Sorry, I'm afraid so," he said and laughed. "I wondered if you would remember."

"When I saw you, I thought I'd met you before, but I couldn't think of when that might have been. Then Max told me that my mother took me up to the Cardwell Ranch for a short visit when I was about nine." She groaned. "Your mother must have been horrified by what I did to you." Jinx didn't think she could be more embarrassed.

He shook his head. "My mother said, 'What

did you do, Angus?' I confessed that I'd been giving you a hard time and that you'd warned me what would happen if I didn't knock it off."

"Oh, I can imagine what my mother said."

"Actually, both mothers had trouble hiding smiles, once they realized that no one was hurt badly. Your mother told you that you couldn't go around pushing boys just because of something they said or you'd spend the rest of your life fighting them."

"You'd think I'd have learned that lesson."

He grinned. "When your mother said that, you replied, 'Well, if the boys are smart, they won't give me a hard time—especially standing in front of an open window two floors up.'"

She laughed with him. "Oh, that sounds so much like me. I'm so sorry."

"Don't be," he said as he seemed to fondly touch the scar. "It was a good learning experience for me." His blue eyes hardened. "And I never forgot that girl."

"I suppose not." She shook her head in disbelief. "Still, you came down to help me get my herd up to summer range."

"Like I said, it's what neighbors do," he said and grinned again. "Also, I was curious to see the woman that girl had grown into."

She couldn't help the heat that rushed to her

cheeks wanting to blame it on the sun beating down on them. "Now you know."

He smiled. "Yes. I wasn't disappointed." He leaned toward her and she knew even before his lips brushed hers, that he was going to kiss her—and she was going to let him.

The kiss started out soft, sweet, delicate, but as her lips parted for him, he looped his hand behind her neck and pulled her down for a proper kiss. She felt the warmth of his bare chest against her still-damp Western shirt. A shiver moved through her as he deepened the kiss. She touched the hair curling at the nape of his neck, wanting to bury her fingers in his dark hair, wanting the kiss to never stop.

At the sound of Max ringing the chow bell, he let her go. She drew back, shaken by the kiss. "We shouldn't have done that."

"I'm not going to apologize for kissing you. I've wanted to since the first time I laid eyes on you. Only back then, I was just a boy who thought the way to get a girl's attention was to give her a hard time."

"I'm still a married woman," she said, hating that she sounded breathless. Had she ever been kissed like that? "And I'm your boss."

He nodded. "If you're saying that I have bad timing, I couldn't agree more." He grinned. "But I'm still not sorry." With that, he touched her cheek, a light caress before he rose, retrieved his shirt from the tree, pulled on his boots and left, saying, "I'll see you back in camp, boss."

JINX WATCHED HIM GO. Her face still felt hot, her cheeks flushed, and her heart was still doing loop-de-loops in her chest. She touched her lips with her fingertips, remembering the feel of his mouth on hers, and couldn't help but smile. Of course the kiss had been wrong. But she was glad that Angus hadn't apologized for it.

As he disappeared into the pines, she couldn't remember ever feeling this good. This free. And if she was being truthful, it hadn't been the first time she'd thought about kissing Angus. He was handsome as the devil. Just the image of his broad chest as he'd come out of the stream, the water rippling over taut, tanned muscles... She shivered, realizing that she wanted more than just a kiss.

That, too, surprised her because for months she hadn't given men, let alone sex, a thought. But that Angus had released this in her, didn't surprise her. She liked him, trusted him, felt close to him. Now that she knew about their earlier connection, she thought with a laugh. But Angus was also the kind of man her father would have approved of. Too bad he hadn't come along before T.D.

Shaking her head, she reminded herself of the mess her life was in right now. She was a woman who'd foolishly married a handsome, smooth-talking man. Now she was living a bad country song, she thought as she rose and pulled on her boots.

The best thing she could do, she told herself, was to keep her distance from Angus. The cattle would be settled into summer range by tomorrow. Once they reached the ranch, he would no longer be in her employ.

But didn't that mean he would be headed home to Montana? He'd told her he was going back to help run Cardwell Ranch. It was just as well, she knew. She certainly wasn't ready for even a man like Angus.

But she felt a shiver as she thought of the way he'd cupped the back of her neck, drawing her down as he deepened the kiss. She found herself smiling again.

She pulled her long hair up into a ponytail and tried not to think about Angus or the kiss or her uncertain future. He would return to Cardwell Ranch. She would sort out the mess she'd made of her life.

Her cheeks still felt hot, though, and she could still taste him on her lips. One look at her and would everyone know when she returned to camp? She realized that she didn't care.

T.D. had failed in his attempt to get the mountain on fire and scatter her herd. She felt ready for whatever else he had up his sleeve, determined to get through this or die trying. Soon she would be free of him. Her step felt lighter as she followed the smell of freshly baked biscuits.

ANGUS HAD WALKED away from Jinx, telling himself to be careful. He thought about the last woman he'd let get this close and how that had turned out. Jinx…well, she was a whole different rodeo in so many ways, including, he reminded himself, that she was married with a crazy not-yet-ex-husband.

He finished buttoning up his shirt. It had dried nicely. As he neared the camp, his brother stepped out of the trees.

"Have a nice swim?" Brick asked, grinning.

"I did." He saw his brother look past him toward the creek. "Don't even think about it."

Brick gave him his best innocent face. "I don't know what you're talking about."

"Jinx. She isn't some prize to be won. She's got serious problems and is in no shape to even think about getting involved with another man."

Brick cocked his head. "Is that what you keep telling yourself?"

Angus sighed. "We're almost done here. Once

the cattle are in the high country, there will be nothing keeping us here."

His brother shook his head. "And you'll just be able to leave her knowing that her jackass of a husband isn't through tormenting her?" He didn't give Angus time to answer. "That's what I thought. You don't want a part of this, brother, trust me. How do you even know that she's over him?"

He thought about the kiss still tingling on his lips. Jinx was over T.D., that he was sure of. But that didn't mean that she was ready for another relationship, especially after her last one. "I'll cross that bridge when I come to it, but you definitely won't have to stay. You and Ella can go back home and—"

Brick was shaking his head. "The three of us signed on and the three of us will leave together. You stay here and you'll get yourself killed."

He wanted to argue that his twin didn't know squat, but unfortunately, Brick was right. He would only make things worse if he stayed. But how could he leave knowing the kind of trouble Jinx was in?

"I just hate to see you falling for her," Brick said. "You're dead right that she's not ready for another man. Hell, she hasn't gotten rid of the one she has."

"There's no reason to be talking about this,"

Angus said as he started past his brother. "Let's just get these cattle safely up to the high country. That's the job we're being paid for. That's enough to worry about since I really doubt that T.D. and his friends are through with us."

His twin caught his arm to stop him. "I'm just worried about you, Angus."

"Maybe it's time you quit worrying about me."

Brick laughed. "We're brothers. Womb mates. I'm going to worry especially when I see you headed down a dangerous path. You just can't stand to see a woman who needs rescuing and not try to rescue her. It's in your DNA. But you almost got killed the last time you got involved in a domestic situation that wasn't any of your business."

He'd gotten between his girlfriend and her former boyfriend, a mistake in so many ways. "This is different."

"Is it? Jinx can divorce T.D., give him what he wants and be done with him. But maybe she's dragging her feet on the property settlement because she is still in love with him. Like you said, she needs time to figure it all out."

"I know that," he said as he stepped past his brother and started again toward camp. He glanced back. It had crossed his mind that Brick might go down to the creek. But to his surprise, his brother now followed him.

"He'll hit us again," Brick said, thankfully changing the subject. "Maybe we *should* try to find him no matter what Jinx says."

"We can't leave the camp unprotected. Jinx is right. With two of us gone, it would be a perfect time for T.D. to strike."

Brick said nothing, but Angus could tell his brother was chewing it over. He just hoped Brick didn't do anything impulsive.

WYATT THOUGHT ABOUT riding out of the mountains and not looking back. T.D. had sent him out to see what damage had been done to Jinx and her herd after the fire. He hated to report that Jinx and her crew had put out the fire with the rainstorm finishing the job. He knew that news was going to put T.D. into a tailspin. He'd thought he was so smart starting the fire.

"Well?" T.D. demanded as he dismounted. "Took you long enough. I thought I was going to have to come look for you."

Wyatt already anticipated the cowboy's reaction to what he had to tell him. "They fought the fire, putting it almost out. Then the rain did the rest. The fire's out."

"What about the herd?" T.D. demanded. "Surely it scattered some of them."

He shook his head. "Sorry."

T.D. swore and stomped around the wet camp.

Royce was trying to get a fire going again but everything was soaking wet after the squall that had come through. He and Cash were arguing, Cash saying he was hungry and might ride down to town.

"We should all ride out of here," Travis said, watching them. He looked wet and miserable. "I don't know what we're doing up here anyway."

T.D. turned on him so quickly Travis didn't have a chance to react. The blow sent him sprawling onto the wet ground. "I'm sick of your whining. Nothing is keeping you here and while you're at it, take those two with you."

Royce looked up, seeming surprised that T.D. meant him and Cash. He'd managed to get a small blaze going. He continued building the fire. Cash, Wyatt noted, had gone silent.

"That's all you saw?" T.D. asked as Wyatt hung up his slicker on a tree limb to dry in the sun. "I thought for sure that the fire would spook the herd. Or at least scatter them."

Wyatt shook his head. All the way back, he'd debated telling T.D. what he'd seen through his binoculars near the stream. Maybe it would end this once and for all. Or maybe it would make T.D. even crazier.

He had no idea what T.D. would do if he told him that he'd seen Jinx and one of her wranglers down by the stream swimming together, then talking while sitting in the sun and then kissing.

Wyatt had watched, unable to pull his eyes away. The two had been so close, so intimate. He wouldn't have been surprised if they'd stripped down and made love right there beside the water. The scene had been so passionate, it had made him wonder if the kiss was the first between the two of them.

He saw that Travis had gotten to his feet and was now busying himself hanging his wet clothing on a tree branch, his back to the rest of them. After T.D. had punched him, why hadn't Travis left? Wyatt told himself he would have gone with him, but he knew that was a lie. T.D. would expect him to stay. Even if he wouldn't, Wyatt wasn't finished up here, was he?

After what he'd seen, he'd been telling himself that Jinx deserved what she was going to get. She was cheating on T.D. Not that it was his place to do anything about that, Wyatt told himself. But if he told T.D., he knew the cowboy would go ballistic, riding up to the camp, guns blazing.

He thought of Patty and the promise she'd made him—and the one he'd kind of made her. T.D. was pacing, worked up because his fire had fizzled out and his attempt to hurt Jinx had failed. So far, nothing that anyone had done had stopped the woman. Suddenly, T.D. stopped pacing and looked at him. "We're going to have to stampede the herd."

Travis turned to glance back at him, but then quickly turned away again. Royce threw a handful of dry dead pine needles onto the fire. "Count me in," he said. Cash just looked uncomfortable but nodded.

Wyatt realized that everyone was waiting on him, including T.D. He told himself that now was the time to put an end to this if he was going to. If he rode back to town now, he suspected the others would follow. He knew Travis was just looking for an excuse to bail but wouldn't unless someone else did first.

He could stop this before it was too late.

Before anyone got killed.

Chapter Eleven

"Hey! Watch out!"

Patty felt the plates of food she'd been carrying tilt dangerously as she collided with one of
the café customers. "Sorry."

The man was busily looking at his sleeve and
then his pants to make sure that none of the café's
evening special had spilled on him. Patty heard
his wife say from the booth, "It was your fault.
You got up right in front of her."

"Are you kidding?" the man demanded. "She
wasn't watching where she was going. If you'd
been paying attention, you would know that she's
been in a daze this whole time. She screwed up
the orders at that other table."

"Seems one of us has been watching the waitress with a little too much interest," the wife
snapped.

Patty felt the heat of embarrassment on the
back of her neck as she delivered the orders to
a far table. The man was right. Her mind hadn't

been on work for some time now. She put on her plastic smile, tried to say all the right things, but she was only going through the motions and at least one person had noticed.

"Everything all right?" her boss asked when she returned to the kitchen.

She had no idea. "Fine." Her mind was in the mountains with T.D. Had he caught up to his wife? For all she knew, the two of them could have made up. She kept seeing a campfire and the two of them rolling around on a bedroll next to it. The image burned through her stomach like acid.

Not that she believed it. Jinx wouldn't take him back. There was no way the two of them were reconnecting, not with all those others up there on the mountain with them. Not only did Jinx have wranglers working for her apparently, but she also had several hundred head of cattle to tend to. She wasn't rolling around with T.D. on any bedroll.

But not knowing what was happening was driving her crazy. Wouldn't she have heard if T.D. and the others had returned to town? Of course she would have. Which meant they hadn't.

So T.D. was still up there in the mountains. Which meant Wyatt was still up there, as well. For a while, she'd forgotten about that.

She thought of the promise she'd made him— and what she'd asked him to do. She'd seen the way he reacted to her. He would do anything for her—just as he'd said. Just as she'd known he would.

A thought made her heart begin to pound.

By now Jinx could be dead.

Unless Wyatt chickened out.

She went to pick up an order for a table that had just come up and tried to still her nervous anticipation. Wyatt wouldn't let her down.

"DON'T YOU THINK we should call the sheriff on T.D.?" Ella asked as she joined her cousins around the campfire later that evening. Max was busy in the chuckwagon and Jinx was seeing to her horse.

They'd spent the day moving cattle, getting as far as they could. Tomorrow was their last day. They should reach summer range before noon, Jinx had said. "And tell him what? I'm sure he knows T.D. followed us up here, but there was little he could do. It's a free country and a huge mountain range," Brick said.

"Brick's right. Nor can we prove he started the fire," Angus said. "I'm not even sure the sheriff could arrest him on the restraining order. T.D. hasn't gotten close enough to break it yet. Also, Jinx said we wouldn't be able to get cell phone service until we reached the high country above the tree line and even then, she said it would be sketchy."

She knew they were right and yet she couldn't

shake the bad feeling she had. "You know he's not finished."

"He'll hit us tonight. He has to," Brick said. "This time tomorrow we'll be in Jackson Hole. I don't know about the two of you, but I plan to kick up my heels. But first I'm going to treat myself to a big fat juicy beef steak and all the fixings. Maybe find me some sweet-smelling woman who wants to dance."

Ella shook her head. "I wouldn't be counting your chickens just yet."

"She's right," Angus agreed. "I don't think the fire did the kind of damage T.D. was hoping for. Whatever he has planned it will be tonight and I suspect it will be much bigger."

Ella poked the fire with a stick, sending sparks into the air. "I don't get why he's doing this. Just to torment her?"

Angus shrugged. "I'm not sure T.D. has a point. He's angry, probably drunk most of the time and feeling he has to do something to save face."

"It's stupid and dangerous," Brick said. "If that fire had gotten away from us or that rain squall hadn't come through when it did…" He shook his head. "The cowboy's crazy."

At the sound of someone coming out of the darkness, they all turned. "Brick's right. T.D. is crazy, stupid and dangerous," Jinx said. "That's why we aren't going to get much sleep tonight."

"I still think we should pay him a visit," Brick said.

"Don't you think they're expecting that?" Ella asked only to have her cousin shrug.

"Also, there's five of them now," Angus said, having earlier seen them trailing the herd. It didn't surprise him that Cash had joined their ranks. "Riding into their camp would be more dangerous than staying where we are and waiting for them to hit us."

"Except we have several hundred head of cattle," Ella said. "If I were him, I'd try to use them against us."

Jinx looked over at her and nodded. "My thought exactly. He'll try to stampede the herd tonight when he thinks we're all asleep. He'll drive them right at us."

"Unless we stop him," Brick said. "That's why we have to hit him first."

Ella saw that Angus was studying Jinx and smiling as if they'd just shared a secret. "You have a plan?"

"Once it's dark enough where we can't be seen, we booby-trap one side of the perimeter," Angus said and Jinx gave him a knowing smile.

Brick caught the exchange and said, "Bro, why

do I get the feeling you told her about what we used to do when we were kids to catch critters?"

"Subject must have come up some time or another," Angus said.

"They have us outnumbered," Jinx said, clearly warming to the plan. "We have to better our odds. I suspect they'll come riding in fast, yelling and shooting to spook the herd. To drive the herd right at us, they'll come in from the north. We just need to be waiting for them, subdue the ones we catch and quell the attack. Any we can get on the ground, should be fairly easy to tie up and gag, right?"

Brick laughed. "I like the way you think. Less bloodshed."

"Hopefully, no blood will be shed." She looked at Angus. "It's going to be another dark night. We weren't going to get any sleep anyway. At least this way we'll be ready for them."

Unless we're wrong and T.D. came at us another way, Ella thought. She wondered how far she'd have to ride to get cell phone coverage should things go as wrong as she feared they would.

"You mind staying here with Max and making sure everything is all right?" Angus asked her as the others rose to go to work.

Ella nodded, knowing exactly what he was telling her to do.

THEY WORKED QUICKLY and quietly, setting up the traps some distance from the herd in the path T.D. would have to take to stampede the cattle into their camp.

Angus checked with Brick to make sure he was ready before he went to the spot where they'd left Jinx. He let out a soft whistle as he approached to let her know it was him coming through the trees and was careful not to trip any of the booby traps.

"You ready?" he asked when he reached her. He could tell she was nervous. They all were. "It's going to be all right."

She smiled. She really did have the most beautiful warm smile. There was a gentleness to her along with strength. He found himself drawn to her in a way he hadn't ever been with another woman. He didn't believe in love at first sight and yet he hadn't forgotten how taken he was with that redheaded girl who'd turned up at Cardwell Ranch, all those years ago.

He touched her cheek, unable to stop himself any more than he could hold back the feelings that swam to the surface when he saw her. He felt connected to her in a way he couldn't explain. He would have said fate had thrown them together not once but twice, years apart, if he believed in it.

Ella would have understood what he was feeling better than he did. She believed in a lot of things he didn't including love at first sight and destiny and true love. But this feeling was so strong that had he believed in true love, he would have been tempted to call it that.

Brick always said that falling in love was like falling off a horse. You had no choice but to get back on. Well, Angus much preferred falling off a horse. To him, falling in love was like jumping off a cliff and not knowing if you would survive. He knew one thing. The landing could be hell.

He'd survived his last breakup, but even as strongly as he felt, he knew he wasn't ready to make another leap. Especially if that leap involved Jinx McCallahan, he told himself. Even if she wasn't married and in the middle of a divorce and didn't have a crazy, dangerous ex who wouldn't let her go. Jinx was a mess. It didn't matter that she'd kicked T.D. out months ago, filed for divorce and didn't want him back under any circumstances, apparently. Her husband wasn't through with her yet. Angus feared she might lose more than her ranch because of T.D.

"Is everything all right?" Jinx asked quietly, no doubt seeing the battle going on inside him.

"Fine," he lied. "How about you?"

"Fine."

He could see that she was as confused as he was. "We're going to get through this," he said, hoping what he was saying was true.

"I hope so," she said as if she knew he didn't just mean tonight.

He was so close, he could see the pain in her face even in the darkness. He knew what it felt like to have a failed relationship. His hadn't even involved getting to the altar. His relationship hadn't lasted that long. But he recalled the pain quite easily. He knew that Jinx wasn't ready for another man any more than he was ready for another woman.

He breathed in the cold mountain air, feeling tired from a long day in the saddle and working hard to get the traps set. It wouldn't be long now. He should get back to his spot.

Yet, he didn't want to leave her. A premonition? He was worried about her and would be until she was free of T.D. In the meantime, he knew she would stay in his thoughts. What was it about her? Those few seconds when she let down her guard and let him see how vulnerable she was? At those moments it took all his strength and good sense not to step to her and take her in his arms, everyone be damned if they didn't like it.

"I should go," he said. Her ex was going to show up at any time. Crazy bitter and probably drunk, nothing good was going to come out of it when T.D. did strike again.

Every time a lock of her coppery hair came loose from her braid and fell over those big brown eyes, he wanted to push it aside. But he knew if he touched her, he'd kiss that mouth again with its bow-shaped full lips.

He realized the trail his thoughts had taken and reined them in with a groan. His brother was right. Something about this woman had him twisted into a knot. His gaze followed her whenever she was around. He couldn't quit thinking about her.

Worse, if he was being honest with himself, he'd been smitten with Jinx from the moment he'd laid eyes on her when they were nothing but kids. It had only gotten worse when he'd seen her again. He recalled the way she'd come out of her house that night at the ranch, shotgun in hand, facing down her ex with courage and determination. She'd shown a strength that had chipped away a corner of his ice-encased heart.

Since being on the cattle drive, he'd felt his heart melting at just the sight of her. She refused to show weakness even when he knew she had to be as exhausted as he was at the end of the day. More and more he felt drawn to her in a way that made him both scared and exhilarated.

He felt like one of the bears that had come out of a long hibernation. He was hungry again in a way he'd never experienced before. Bad timing be damned. He wanted this woman.

JINX SHIVERED IN the darkness. She was so close to Angus that she could look into his blue eyes. This was it, she thought. They could all die tonight. She yearned for Angus to take her in his arms.

He brushed a lock of her hair back from her face. She felt her eyes widen, but she didn't move. "Why are you looking at me like that?"

"I'm counting your freckles. I've wanted to since I first laid eyes on you," he whispered, so close now that she could hardly breathe.

She smiled to hide how nervous it made her. "I take it you have a lot of time to kill?"

He met her gaze and smiled. "Not as much as I'd like right now," he whispered. "You don't have any idea how beautiful you are."

She chuckled self-consciously and dropped her gaze. "Angus—"

With his warm fingers, he lifted her chin until their eyes locked. "You're beautiful, Jinx, and I haven't been able to take my eyes off you this whole time."

Her pulse jumped as he bent to brush his lips over hers. The heat of her desire rushed through her veins, hot as liquid lava. She'd never felt this kind of need before, knowing only one man could satisfy it.

Angus pulled back to look into her eyes for a moment before he dropped his mouth to hers again. She surrendered to his kiss as he parted her lips and delved deeper. His arms came around her, pulling her against him until she could feel the beat of his heart in sync with her own.

She opened to him, no longer fighting her feelings. Desire flared, his kisses fanning the flames. She lost herself in his kisses, in the strength of his arms drawing her to him, in the low moan she heard escape his lips as she pulled back.

"Jinx," he whispered her name on a ragged breath. "Jinx." Angus said it low, soft, a caress that sent a pleasurable shiver across her skin. Then his fingers touched her face, drawing her closer until she was looking into his eyes, losing herself in them.

His mouth was dropping to hers again. Her lips parted, as if there had been no doubts between them. One arm looped around her waist, pulling her into his solid body. She felt his need as much as her own. Like her, she knew that he feared tonight might be their last.

She surrendered to him, needing this man's strength as well as his gentleness. What surprised her was the fire he set ablaze inside her. T.D. had never ignited such passion. He'd been rough and demanding, believing that was what every woman wanted.

Angus seemed to know what she needed, what she desperately desired, as if he knew instinctively that she hadn't been truly satisfied. Because of that, she felt vulnerable and exposed. Had it been any other man other than Angus…

His breathing was as labored as her own as his hand slipped up under her coat to her warm flesh. She arched against him, wanting and needing more, as she let out a moan of pure pleasure and whispered his name.

They both froze at a sound in the trees lower on the mountain. For a while, she'd completely forgotten T.D., forgotten everything but the feel of this cowboy's arms around her.

Angus groaned quietly and let go of her, drawing back. "When this is over," he said on a hoarse breath. "Jinx, I promise, when this is over…"

She touched her finger to his lips and shook her head. They couldn't make promises. Not tonight. Not under these circumstances.

Angus looked as if he couldn't bear to leave her. She knew the feeling. She gave him a gentle shove.

Nearby, they heard one of the traps being sprung. Then silence.

ANGUS WAS FURIOUS with himself as he rushed back to his spot on the mountain only to find that a deer had tripped one of his traps. The pretty doe bound off into the distance. But it could have just as easily been T.D. or one of his men.

He shouldn't have left his traps unattended. He wouldn't again.

He'd let himself get carried away. It wasn't like him and yet when he'd looked at Jinx... He thought of what he'd seen in her eyes. A need like his own. A fear matching his own. Tonight everything could go wrong and there could be bloodshed.

Forcing that thought away, he told himself it was why they'd both been vulnerable. Just the thought of the two of them on the side of this mountain in the dark and what he'd wanted to happen... He knew it was insane, but he'd felt as if they were the last two people in the world. Neither of them had wanted to stop, but fortunately, when the deer tripped the trap, they had.

What if it had been T.D. instead of a deer? What if he'd seen the two of them? He shook his head at his own impetuousness, let alone his foolishness. He could have gotten both Jinx and himself killed.

Tomorrow they would reach her grazing land with the herd, then... But that was the problem. Then Jinx would be back at her ranch dealing with her problems and there would be no excuse for him to hang around. That was if they lived through tonight, he reminded himself.

He heard a meadowlark whistle close by. "You all right?" Brick whispered as he came out of the darkness of the pines. "I heard one of your traps go off."

"Deer. A little doe." His voice sounded strange even to him.

"You all right?" his brother asked suspiciously.

"Just jumpy. You should get back to your traps."

He nodded but didn't move for a moment. Angus wondered if his twin could tell from his expression even in the darkness what he'd been up to.

"We'll be done tomorrow," Brick said.

"I was just thinking about that," he said, honestly.

"I bet you were."

"I'm looking forward to going home to the ranch."

"Glad to hear that." Brick slapped him on the shoulder. "Be careful."

"You, too." He watched his brother disappear back through the pines and tried to concentrate on staying alive tonight.

Chapter Twelve

As they waited for the cover of darkness, T.D. thought about sneaking into camp, finding his wife and collecting on at least some of what she owed him. She hadn't just kicked him off the ranch. She'd kicked him out of her bed months ago.

He'd been fine with it at the time. He'd had Patty, and Patty was always willing. But she wasn't Jinx. Patty couldn't fill a need in him that had little to do with sex. Jinx had filled that need. He'd been married to her and the ranch. He'd felt he finally belonged somewhere.

What bothered him was that he'd thought Jinx would come begging for him after a few weeks, let alone a few months, without him.

But she hadn't. It seemed impossible that she hadn't seemed to miss his lovemaking as if he hadn't been giving her what she needed. Was that true? If so, it shook the very foundation of what he believed about himself. All he'd ever had was

his looks and his way with women. That Jinx
might have found him lacking drove him insane
with fury.

Patty never complained, he told himself. And
yet the fact that Jinx didn't want him back ate at
him. When he got the chance again, he'd remind
Jinx what she'd been missing.

"Let's get ready to go," he ordered everyone
gathered around the fire. He sensed they weren't
as into this as he was and that annoyed him.

"Don't you think she's going to be expecting
this?" Travis asked without moving.

He didn't bother to answer him. Travis was
right about one thing, though. Jinx knew him
too well. She'd know he'd come for her tonight,
their last night on this mountain. But not even
Travis knew what he had planned. In the dark
there would be confusion. At least that was his
hope. Jinx would anticipate what he had planned.
Too bad there was nothing she could do about it,
though.

Still, it made him wonder if he was too predictable. Is that why she thought she could live without him? Maybe it was time to prove to her that
he could still surprise her. He smiled to himself.

"Here's what I want you all to do," he said and
told them their part of the plan, keeping his own
to himself. He knew he couldn't depend on Travis
or Royce or Cash. But at least he had Wyatt here

with him. They'd been buds since grade school. Wyatt would have his back.

Stepping away from the dying coals of the campfire, he pulled his binoculars from where he'd left his saddlebag to look toward her camp. He couldn't see a damned thing, it was so dark tonight. He thought about last night when he'd spotted Jinx and he'd felt his pulse jump like it always did when he caught her unawares.

She'd been standing not far from the light of their campfire. He'd been studying her when he realized that she wasn't alone. His heart had begun to pound wildly. He'd felt weak with shock and fury. She'd stood talking to one of her wranglers—the same one who'd come to her rescue back down at the ranch.

He'd seen the way she was standing, the way she had her head tilted to look up at the cowboy. She liked him. Maybe more than liked him. He realized that he hadn't even considered what his wife had been doing all these months when she wasn't letting him into her bed. How many other wranglers had there been since she'd kicked him out? Did everyone in the county know what had been going on but him?

His blood had pounded so hard in his head, he'd felt dizzy.

That was when he knew that he could kill her. She'd humiliated him for the last time. When he'd seen her standing with that cowboy, he could have grabbed his rifle and taken a shot right then, but suddenly a cold calm had come over him. As his wife had stepped away from the cowboy, he'd lowered the binoculars. For possibly the first time in his life, he hadn't gone off half-cocked. He was going in prepared this time because now he knew what had to be done.

He would find her while the others kept everyone else busy. He'd find her and finish this.

ELLA PUT OUT the campfire as planned and watched the smoke rise slowly into the darkness. Quiet fell over the mountainside. The plan had been to make everything seem as it had been other nights. As predicted, clouds had rolled in, smothering any starlight tonight.

She listened, knowing it wouldn't be long before this moment of peace was interrupted. Brick, Jinx and Angus had left to be ready. Jinx was closest to camp but Ella couldn't see her. She thought about their traps. They didn't have time to dig holes or pits, but would use the pine tree boughs to make a swinging log that could be released as a rider passed. Another one would have a large rock that swung down from a tree.

"Even if some of them miss, they will be enough of a distraction that we can attack," Brick had said, clearly enjoying this.

"We need to immobilize as many of them as we can before they reach the herd," Jinx had said.

Ella had opted to stay in camp to set up some booby traps of her own just in case the others were wrong about how and where T.D. would strike.

"You're a smart woman," Max said now as he left behind his beloved chuckwagon to take refuge in an outcropping of trees next to a wall of rock some distance from the camp. She'd talked him into it, wanting him out of the line of fire no matter what happened tonight.

"You should have a good view from there," Ella had said as she'd tried to sell him on the idea. "But you'll also be armed so if any of them decide to come this way…"

The older man nodded, clearly seeing what she was up to. "I would love to get that man in my sights."

She gave him a disapproving look. "We're supposed to wound them unless we have no other options."

"I'll be sure to keep that in mind."

Leaving him, she went back to where the campfire had died to nothing but a tiny stream of smoke before climbing into the chuckwagon to get the pots and pans she needed. Her trap wasn't lethal, but it would alert them if T.D. and his men were circling around behind them. Max would be safe as long as he stayed out of sight.

ANGUS FINISHED THE last of the swinging branch booby traps and looked through the trees to where he could barely see Jinx. He knew that like him, she was waiting and listening. Jinx thought that T.D. would come roaring in, all liquored up, shooting and yelling and out of control.

They wouldn't have any trouble hearing them coming, if that was the case. Jinx didn't expect T.D. to approach this rationally. She just assumed he would be drunk, angry and acting out rather than having a plan.

But Angus thought that she might be wrong and that expecting him to act as he usually did could be a mistake. T.D. knew this was his last night to stop them from reaching summer range—or at least cost them another day or so, if he scattered the herd. So Angus stood listening, suspecting T.D. would try to sneak up on them instead.

He couldn't help but worry. Ella had stayed back at camp to take care of things there. She'd looked worried but he knew she would take care of Max and herself.

They were all worried, he thought, as on impulse, he moved quietly through the pines to where Jinx was waiting. He drew her into his arms, unable to fight the bad feeling that had overcome him. She leaned into him as if glad to let him take some of the weight off her—at least for a moment.

At the sound of something moving slowly, cautiously toward them, they separated. Brick came out of the darkness, whispering, "Is it safe?"

Angus wasn't sure if he meant from the booby traps or because he had spotted Jinx in his brother's arms. "We're as ready as we can be."

Brick nodded. "I'm going back up the mountain to my spot." He pulled some strips of leather from his jacket pocket. "If I get one down, I'll make sure he won't be any more trouble until I untie him at daylight." He pulled out the wad of torn dish towels he planned to use as gags. His brother gave him a grin before disappearing back up the mountainside.

Angus just hoped this worked and that no one got hurt or worse, killed. But that would be up to T.D., he thought with a shudder as the darkness seemed to take on a life of its own. "They're coming," he whispered as he heard a horse whinny in the distance.

Chapter Thirteen

As Brick hurried back up the mountainside, Angus returned to his spot. Jinx could tell he hadn't wanted to leave her. The night felt colder not being in his arms. She tried to concentrate on what had to be done, rather than the wrangler.

With luck, this would work. Even if T.D. stampeded the cattle into their camp, the only thing that would be destroyed was Max's beloved chuckwagon. A chuckwagon could be replaced. Max, in the meantime, would be safe away from camp, Ella had assured her.

She knew they were as ready as possible and still she couldn't help being scared. With a man like T. D. Sharp… Had he followed her up here just to torment her? To keep her from getting her herd to summer range? Or was his motive even more treacherous? She remembered the look in his eyes the other night at the ranch and knew at that moment, he'd wished her dead.

Jinx swallowed the lump in her throat, telling

herself the man didn't scare her even as she knew it wasn't true. There was something about him, a feeling that he'd stepped over some invisible barrier and now he felt he had nothing to lose. If he ever got her alone again...

She shivered and pushed the thought away. His attack on them tonight would get him sent to jail. At least temporarily. With luck, she could get a loan against the ranch until she had it sold. Dangling that kind of money in front of T.D., she thought she could get him to sign the divorce papers. She wanted this over.

Right now the thought of losing the ranch didn't seem so overpowering. Standing here in the dark, trying to gauge what T.D. would do next, she had a whole different set of priorities. She wanted to live. Angus had made her realize there were more important things than a piece of land or a herd of cattle. There could be a life after T.D., after losing her mother and father, after even losing the ranch.

Not that she was ready for that life. Not that Angus might even be in it. But he'd made her see that her mistake in marrying T.D. wasn't the end of the world. It was only the end of this life. She could put this all behind her without knowing what the future held for her—just that she had one.

If she lived past tonight.

Waiting in the dark, the night getting colder, she regretted her own stubbornness. She should have sold her cattle, taken a loss and put the ranch up for sale. She'd put not just her life in jeopardy. Now Angus, Brick and Ella along with Max were in danger because she was so damned determined to get the herd to summer range.

As much as she hated to admit it, she'd done it not just out of stubbornness. She'd wanted to show T.D. that he wasn't going to run her life, let alone ruin it. Her stubborn pride could get them all killed. She couldn't bear the thought. Angus, Brick and Ella had answered her ad because Dana and Jinx's mother had been close. They should never have had to come all this way. None of them should be on this mountainside right now knowing there was a madman out there in the pines set on vengeance.

Another horse whinnied from deep in the pines above her on the mountain. She heard a branch snap under a horse's hoof. They were moving more slowly than she'd expected. Did they expect a trap?

She pulled the weapon at her hip, hoping she wouldn't have to use it. The plan had been to cause enough confusion to drive them back— if not subdue any who fell into their traps. By cutting down their numbers, it would make T.D. think twice. At least that was the hope. She knew he was basically a coward. He needed his two close friends to bolster his courage—that and alcohol.

Unfortunately, he had them and two more men who would follow his orders if he offered them the right incentives.

The sound of the riders grew closer. She could hear the creak of saddle leather, the brush of tree boughs and whisper of high grass against the horses' legs as their riders kept coming.

Jinx found herself holding her breath. She knew how quickly everything could go south. Behind her, the cattle lowed softly. If she was right, the approaching riders would begin firing their weapons and yelling as they tried to stampede the herd back toward the camp.

And if she was wrong?

ANGUS FELT THE hair rise on the back of his neck as he realized the riders had spread out and at least one would soon be almost on top of him. Even in the pitch blackness of the spring night, he waited for the shapes to materialize out of the dark.

The trick, he knew, was to stay calm until it was time to attack. The booby traps were springloaded. All a horse had to do was trip the rope hidden in the tall green grass and all hell would break loose. Jinx could handle this, he told himself. At the same time he was reminded that all of this was about her.

T.D. had ridden all the way up here with his friends to cause her trouble. He wanted to torment her. To make her pay for not taking him back. To hurt her.

And that was what scared Angus the most. If T.D. got his hands on her, how far would the man go?

He couldn't see her through the trees, but he knew she was still there. He hadn't wanted to leave her alone, still didn't.

A swishing sound off to his left on the mountainside was followed by a cry of pain. He could hear what sounded like a struggle, then silence. He listened hard for the all-clear signal and finally heard his brother whistle a meadowlark's call.

He tried to relax. Brick had one of them down. Four to go.

The riders seemed to be quickening their pace through the pines. One of his log swings snapped in the darkness. He heard an *oouft* sound followed by a loud thump as a body hit the ground. An instant later, a horse ran past him—sans its rider.

Angus sprang into action, moving quickly toward where he'd heard the man fall. As he neared, he heard mewing sounds. Gun drawn, he pounced on the man only to have him cry out in pain.

"My arm," the man cried. "It's broken." His eyes widened as he saw the gun in Angus's hand. "Don't kill me. None of this was my idea." The man began to cry.

Angus saw that there was no way to tie the man's hands, so he took the man's weapon and tied his ankles together along with the wrist of his good arm.

"You have to get me a doctor," the man pleaded. "I don't want to die out here."

He hurriedly put his hand over the man's mouth. "Where's T.D.?" he asked the man quietly and released his grip on the man's mouth long enough to let him answer.

"I don't know. I thought he was with us, but I haven't seen him since we left camp."

He quickly gagged the man, fearing it was too late. The others could have heard him. But none of them had come to his aid. At least not yet.

In the distance he heard another of the booby traps snap off to his left. Brick had another one down, followed by the meadowlark whistle. As another booby trap went off, he waited but heard nothing. That one must have missed. Or maybe the man had wised up and gotten off his horse.

To Angus's count, they had three down. That left two men. Did Brick have T.D.? If not, was he one of the two left? He hoped they'd heard what was going on and had headed back. He listened, hearing nothing but the pounding of his own heart.

That was until he heard an earsplitting racket coming from camp and then dead silence.

THE FIRST SIGNS of daylight cast an eerie dark gray shadow over the mountainside. From her perch in one of the large old pines, Ella saw that a riderless horse had set off her alarm in the camp. She watched the horse head for the corral where their horses whinnied and moved around restlessly.

So where was the rider? She felt anxious, worried about what was happening in the forest beyond the camp. But she wasn't about to leave Max. She'd promised Jinx she would make sure he was safe.

He sat with his back against the rock rim, his shotgun resting in his lap. She watched from her tree perch. The clouds had parted some. The sky to the east lightened in the area around her, and she wondered how long before dawn. Her eyes felt dry and scratchy from staring into the darkness of the pines.

She listened but heard nothing but the cattle lowing in the meadow higher up the mountain. Closer, she heard the steady beat of her heart as she waited and prayed that the others were all right. And yet as she waited, she feared something had gone wrong. She kept thinking about the horse that had set off her alarm—and its empty saddle. Where was the man who'd been riding it?

JINX TENSED AS she heard the noise coming from camp, but before she could react, she heard a rider bearing down on her. She had her gun ready, hoping she didn't have to use it. A riderless horse burst out of the darkness and ran past her.

She let out the breath she'd been holding and tried to relax. The horse had come from the direction of the camp. She told herself that Ella would take care of whoever had set off the alarm back there—just as she would make sure Max was safe. If she was able.

Listening, Jinx heard nothing. The quiet was more unnerving than the racket had been. She had no idea how many of the men were down. Or if any of them had turned back. All she knew was that unless they had T.D., he was still on this mountain somewhere. Maybe even closer by than she knew. That thought sent a shudder through her. She feared how badly things could go on this mountainside.

The sound of the gunshot made her jump. It had come from higher up on the mountain. *Brick.* Her heart dropped. She knew Angus would go to him. She could hear movement through the pines off to her right. It was still pitch black in the pines, but the sky was lightening in the distance. Soon the sun would rise. Soon she would be able to see who was coming at her.

A closer sound made her freeze. She sensed T.D. even before she heard the swish of his boots through the tall grass behind her, followed by the smell of the alcohol on his breath as she swung around, leading with the pistol in her hand.

T.D. was on her so quickly she didn't have time to even pull the trigger. He covered her mouth with his gloved hand before she could scream as he ripped the pistol from her grip. Tossing the weapon away into the darkness, he put his face against the side of hers and whispered, "Hello, wife. Don't you wish you'd just paid me off when I asked nicely?"

Chapter Fourteen

Angus ran through the pines toward the sound of
the gunshot, knowing where it had come from.
His brother was in trouble. There hadn't been the
meadowlark whistle as hard as he had listened for
it. The clouds had moved off, leaving a lighter
ceiling overhead as daylight peeked through the
pines.

He could make out shapes through the trees.
He saw two horses, both tied to a limb. That
meant three men down, just as he'd thought. He
hadn't heard another trap being sprung. What had
happened that there'd been a gunshot?

Because there were still two men out there, he
reminded himself as he ran through the pines.
He'd known at once that the gun report had come
from the spot where Brick had set up his booby
traps. As he ran, he prayed for the sound of his
brother's meadowlark whistle. But it didn't come
to let him know that Brick was all right. Because
in his heart, he knew he wasn't.

He didn't even consider that he might be running into a trap. All he could think about was getting to his twin. He'd felt that shot as if the bullet had entered his own body. Because they were identical twins, they'd always shared a special bond. Not that they'd dressed alike or were alike in so many ways. They'd never had a special language that was all theirs. Nor had they ever sensed when the other was in trouble. Until now.

Angus was almost to Brick when he heard the second gunshot. He burst through the pines, shoving aside boughs to find his brother lying on the ground next to two bodies. In that instant, he saw that Cash had been gagged and tied up but had managed to free himself.

At the sight of Angus, the man jumped up, ran to his horse and pulling the reins free, took off down the mountain as if the devil himself was after him. On the ground next to Brick, Royce lay dead from a gunshot wound to the chest. There was a gun dangling from the man's fingertips even though his wrists were bound.

He saw what had happened as clearly as if he'd witnessed the whole thing. Royce had pulled a second gun that Brick hadn't found on him before his brother had tied the cowboy up.

Angus dropped down beside his brother. Brick was trying to say something. There was a dark blood spot on his upper chest that was getting larger and darker. Angus quickly pulled off his coat and pressed it to the wound.

As he did, he heard someone coming through the trees. He didn't go for his gun, knowing he wouldn't have time to pull it. He picked up Brick's gun and turned it as the figure burst through the pines.

Ella. He eased his finger off the trigger as she dropped to the ground beside Brick. "Help is on the way," she said as she took over holding the coat to her cousin's wound. "I was able to get cell service from the top of a pine tree."

Angus felt a surge of relief. Help was on the way. But her next words turned his blood to ice.

"I think T.D. has Jinx," she said. "She's not where she's supposed to be and there are drag marks going down the mountain. His horse set off my alarm. I had a bad feeling so I called for help, then climbed down the tree. I was on my way to check when I heard the second shot."

His heart had dropped to his boots. Brick was shot and T.D. had Jinx?

"I'll take care of Brick," his cousin said. "Go find her. Before it's too late."

As T.D. DRAGGED her through the woods, Jinx tried to fight him. He held her by the throat, his boozy breath next to her ear as he told her what he was going to do to her. When he'd first jumped her, he'd thrown her down, knocking the air out of her.

She fought him, scratching and kicking and biting, only to have him slap her so hard she saw stars. He'd sat on her and quickly bound her wrists and gagged her with her bandanna. He'd thought she would scream for help. She could see that T.D. was just hoping someone would come to her rescue so he could kill them.

With his arm locked around her neck, he dragged her. When she tried to fight him, he cut off her airway until she quit struggling. At first she'd been terrified, knowing at least in part, what he planned to do to her. But the more she fought him, the more furious she got. How dare he think he could treat her this way?

She knew she needed to save her strength for when she had a chance of actually getting away from him, but the mad she had going felt good. And it was so much better than terror right now.

He stopped under a large old pine tree far from the camp. Throwing her down, he climbed on top of her. She glared at him, putting all her disgust into the look.

"It's not rape," he said as if reading her gaze clearly enough. "You're still my wife, which means you are still mine to do whatever I want with." His idea of marriage astounded her. She tried to tell him what she thought of him through her gag but he only laughed, not understanding a word.

"Come on, you like this," he said as if he could still charm her. "I love you. I just want to show you how much, remind you of what you've been missing. You have been missing it, haven't you?" His gaze narrowed for a moment. "Don't you remember what it was like with the two of us? You know you still love me. We can stop this right now. All you have to do is admit it was a mistake when you threw me out. It isn't too late for us."

She knew it was a lie, but she wondered if T.D. did. Maybe he believed everything he said. If she submitted to him, it wouldn't be over. Even now, she could see that he didn't trust her. Didn't trust that he could charm her anymore. She could see the fear in his eyes. Even if she were stupid enough to take him back, his anger and insecurity would make their lives a living hell. He'd always said, when he was drinking, that she thought he wasn't good enough for her. He was the one who believed that until he'd proven to her he was right.

T.D. wasn't good enough for her. He wasn't the kind of man she wanted in her life. Not now. Not ever.

He stared at her in the growing light. Was he having second thoughts about this? Was he wishing like she was that none of this had ever happened?

Slowly, he leaned down to kiss her, but she

moved her head from side to side each time he
tried and attempted to buck him off. But he was
too strong for her. She wouldn't submit to him.
She couldn't.

Swearing, he said, "Fine. We don't have much
time so let's get right to it." He unzipped her
coat and then grabbed her Western shirt and un-
snapped it in one quick, hard jerk. "I'll just take
what's mine. You want it rough? Well, too bad,
because that's the way you're getting it."

She'd told herself that she would kill him if he
ever touched her again. He'd bound her wrists
behind her with duct tape and had her lying partially on her side. She felt a little give in the duct
tape. He'd been in a hurry and he hadn't done a
good job.

As he leaned over her, grabbing her chin to
hold her head still while he kissed her hard, she
moved her hands down her side and pulled her
legs up until she could reach her boot with the
knife in it.

Drawing the knife from the sheath, she clutched
it tightly in her fist. She knew she could do little
damage with the knife the way she was bound.
But right now just getting him off her would be
a start. Leaning back, she got the blade between
her wrists and felt it cut through most of the tape.
Just a little more.

T.D. took her movements as her getting into

what was happening. He deepened the kiss as he groped her through her bra. The tape gave. Her wrists free, she swung the knife.

He must have sensed that her hands were free because he moved just enough that the blade cut into his side—rather than his back. He let out a howl of pain, grabbing her wrist with such force that she dropped the blade before she could stab him again. Still on top of her, T.D. snatched up the knife, his blood staining it.

Her breath caught in her throat as he leaned over her, flashing the blade in her face. She closed her eyes as he wiped the blood off on her cheek. "You stupid bitch," he breathed, sounding as if in pain. She knew it was only a flesh wound. She had succeeded in only making him angrier with her.

But she opened her eyes, defiantly glaring at him. If he didn't know before, he did now. She would rather die than let him do this to her.

Holding her wrists down above her head with one hand, he laid the cold knife blade against the bare skin of her chest for a moment, before he cut her bra open. She felt the cold night air on her exposed breasts and heard his chuckle when he saw her puckered nipples.

It's the cold, you idiot, she wanted to say, even more contempt in her gaze.

He recognized it because he growled, "I could cut your throat just as easily."

Please do, she thought.

"Maybe I will cut you, once I'm through with you," he said, so close that she wanted to gag on the alcohol fumes. He pocketed the knife and rolled her over, duct-taping her wrists again, this time more roughly.

Flopping her back over, he held her down with his body as he stared at her for a long moment. She felt a chill because the look was clear. This was goodbye. He would never let her leave this mountain alive.

She heard him unzip his jeans before he began fumbling to get hers undone, shifting to one side as he did. Jinx brought her knee up hard and fast and caught him in the groin. As he let out a howl and leaned to one side, she bucked him the rest of the way off and rolled to the side to scramble to her feet.

He reached for her, grabbing a handful of blue jean fabric and dragging her back. She kicked at him, but he pulled himself to his feet and slapped her so hard she tasted blood.

His voice was hoarse with fury and pain as he locked one arm around her throat again, pulled his pistol and held it to her head. "You're a dead woman."

WYATT TRIED TO hold the rifle steady. His finger brushed over the trigger. All he had to do was pull it. Pull it and Jinx would be history. Patty would be grateful.

At the thought of her, his finger hovered on the trigger. If only he could quit shaking—and get his crosshairs on Jinx. Since the moment T.D. had grabbed Jinx, he hadn't had a clear shot.

Just when he had the crosshairs on her, they both moved. He swore. He could feel himself sweating profusely under his coat even though the early morning was freezing cold. The sky around him was lightening. He had a clear view of the two and wasn't sure how much longer he would.

He hadn't heard any of the others for some time now. Not since the sound of that gunshot had broken the silence. Earlier T.D. had spelled out the plan to them. Even as he was talking, Wyatt knew he was lying. T.D. wanted them to quietly sneak up on the herd before they started shooting and hollering and scattering them.

But just before they left camp, T.D. pulled him aside to tell him that he had a different plan for him. "I'm going to sneak into the camp from the other way, find Jinx and finish this. I want you to cover my back."

Wyatt had nodded numbly, thinking that the cowboy's plan worked out perfectly for his own plan. They'd ridden for a way with the others and then cut off through the pines to ride up almost to the camp. It had been T.D.'s idea to let his horse go into camp as a decoy. The man wasn't stupid. He knew Jinx was expecting the attack.

Wyatt had hung back but kept his eye on T.D.

Now he stood some yards away. The rifle was getting heavy. He didn't know how much longer he could wait to take a shot. Worse, he thought he'd heard a helicopter in the distance.

When he'd lowered the rifle, then lifted it again, he'd been shocked to see that Jinx had almost gotten away from T.D. The rifle wavered in his hands. Surely he hadn't missed his chance at a clean shot.

He fought now to get the crosshairs on her. T.D. had his arm around her neck and a pistol to her head. What the hell? Was he only threatening her? He couldn't believe that this situation might solve itself. If T.D. killed Jinx, he wouldn't have to and yet he could take credit when he saw Patty. T.D. would be going to prison...

Wyatt felt a surge of hope that everything might work out for him. But T.D. had to pull that trigger. He watched as Jinx tried to fight him off. Any moment the wranglers working for her would be coming. What was T.D. thinking, taking this risk? *Shoot her!*

Couldn't the man feel time running out? It struck him that T.D. was crazy. He always had been, but lately he'd been getting worse. He was going to get them all thrown in jail—if not killed.

As he watched through the scope, Wyatt realized that T.D. wasn't going to shoot her. If Jinx was going to die, it would be up to Wyatt to finish this and soon. He'd missed a good shot earlier when he'd lowered the rifle for even a moment and was now mentally kicking himself. This could already be over. He could have killed Jinx.

The rifle wavered in his arms, the crosshairs going from Jinx's face to T.D.'s as the two kept moving around. Wyatt thought of how disappointed Patty would be if he didn't do what had to be done. How disappointed he would be in himself because any hope he had of ever being with Patty would be gone.

Not that T.D. stood a chance now of ever getting Jinx back—and freeing Patty. Hadn't Wyatt been hoping that his friend would return to Jinx and break it off with Patty for good? He could have seen himself comforting the brokenhearted Patty. He'd seen it as a chance to win the woman's heart.

But now it was clear that Jinx was never going back to T.D.—not after this. T.D. had blown any chance he had by following her up here into the mountains. Not that it seemed he stood a chance anyway since now there was a wrangler in the mix. Jinx had moved on—and damned quickly, if he said so himself. Patty thought she had to get rid of Jinx to get T.D. back. Jinx was already long gone.

Through the rifle scope he tried to get a shot at Jinx. T.D. wasn't going to pull the trigger. Instead, his friend seemed to be looking back up the mountain. For a moment Wyatt feared that he'd seen him and almost lowered the rifle. No, T.D. must have heard some of the others coming. Time had run out.

He put the crosshairs on Jinx's red head and assured himself that no one would know who fired the fatal shot. T.D. would be blamed for all of it—not that he wouldn't probably get away with it, just as he had all of their lives. He'd dragged them up on this mountain, gotten him and Travis in trouble, and T.D. would somehow shift the blame.

If T.D. shot Jinx he'd go to prison and Patty would be free. But even as he thought it, Wyatt knew the man didn't have what it took to pull the trigger.

Wyatt settled the crosshairs on Jinx as the sun caught in her red hair. "This is for you, Patty."

As DAWN BROKE over the mountains, Angus followed the drag marks down the mountain at a run, his pistol drawn, his heart racing. He had to find Jinx.

He came to a sliding stop as he saw them—and

they saw him. T.D. pulled her out of the darkness of a large pine, using Jinx like a human shield. She was gagged and from what he could see, her hands seemed to be bound behind her. Her coat was open, along with her shirt, her bare breasts covered by her long hair.

T.D. had a gun to her head and was grinning as he locked his free arm around her neck, pulling her back against him. "Drop your gun or I'll kill her right now," he ordered. "I wouldn't try me on this."

Angus could see the fear in Jinx's face, but suspected that it was more for him than for herself. He felt his finger on the trigger, the barrel pointed at T.D.'s head. But it was a shot he knew he couldn't take.

He thought about what to do as he considered his options. They were limited. He could rush the two of them and hope for the best. There was a desperation in T.D.'s expression. He looked nervous, like a trapped animal, and that made him even more dangerous. The man knew that he'd never get out of this, not this time. Brick had been shot. Royce was dead. T.D. would have heard the gunfire.

What Angus feared was that the man would panic and shoot Jinx if he didn't drop his gun. He slowly lowered his pistol to the ground, knowing that there was nothing stopping T.D. from shooting him.

But Angus was ready. If T.D. even started to pull the gun away from Jinx's head, he was ready to launch himself at the man. There was a good chance he would be shot, but if he could save Jinx, it was a chance he had to take.

"I know she's been with you," T.D. said, anger marring his handsome face. "Just the thought of you and her..." Jinx let out a cry as T.D. tightened his hold on her.

Angus started to take a step forward, but T.D. quickly said, "Don't do it. I'll kill her. You know I will. If I can't have her, then no one can, especially you."

He could tell that Jinx was having trouble breathing. "You don't want to go to prison."

T.D. laughed. "I've been headed there my whole life. The only thing good I ever had was Jinx. And now that's gone." He pressed the pistol barrel harder to her temple, making her wince. "This is all your fault, Jinx. You only have yourself to blame."

The air filled with a sound of a gunshot report.

Chapter Fifteen

Angus started at the sound. He had no idea where the shot had come from—just that it had happened fast. Suddenly Jinx was on the ground and T.D. was standing over her splattered with blood. Angus was instantly moving, grabbing up his gun from the ground as he rushed toward T.D.

Another shot filled the air, biting the bark of a tree next to T.D. as the man turned and ran into the pines. Angus launched himself down the hill to cover Jinx from the gunfire. He still wasn't sure where the shots were coming from or who was firing them. He shielded Jinx, terrified that she was already badly injured by the first gunshot.

"Jinx!" he cried as he hurriedly removed the gag from her mouth. "Jinx?" As the gunfire stopped, he heard someone take off on horseback. Pulling his pocketknife, he cut her wrists free and turned her onto her back to lower her to the soft ground.

Her eyes were open. But like T.D.'s, her face was splattered with blood to the extent that he couldn't tell where she'd been hit.

"Angus," she said, her lips curving into a smile before her eyes closed.

"Jinx, don't leave me. Jinx?" He moved closer. In the growing light of day, he could see where a bullet had grazed her temple. He checked her pulse. It was strong. She didn't seem to have any other injuries, he realized with relief. He could hear a helicopter approaching. Closer, he heard someone moving through the tall grass and trees toward him.

He spun around, pistol ready, and then relaxed. "Max, Jinx has been hit."

Max stumbled up to them and dropped to his knees next to her. Jinx opened her eyes. "Max." The older man took her hand as her gaze shifted to Angus. "T.D.?"

"He got away," he said.

"No," both Max and Jinx said almost in unison.

"A helicopter will be here in just a minute," Max said. "I'll stay with Jinx. Don't let T.D. get away."

Angus saw the worry in the older man's eyes. Unless T.D. was stopped, Jinx would never be safe. He felt torn. He didn't want to leave her, but he damned sure didn't want T.D. to get away.

"Go," Max urged him. "She'll be all right. I'll stay with her and make sure of that."

Swearing, Angus took off down the mountain, following the blood trail T.D. was leaving as the sun topped the mountain and fingered its way through the pines. T.D. hadn't come at them as they'd both anticipated. Instead, he'd sent his flunkies in while he circled around to come up the back way. He'd never planned to stampede the herd. The man had only been after Jinx, letting the others be the diversion he needed.

The bad feeling Angus had had since they'd taken this job had now settled in his bones. He had to find T.D., if it was the last thing he did. As he looked into the dark shadows of the pines, he knew it could very well be just that.

T.D. RAN, SLUMPED over from the pain. He still couldn't believe that Jinx had stabbed him. But that was the least of his worries. He was bleeding from a gunshot wound to his upper chest and because of that, he was leaving a trail. Worse, he knew someone was behind him coming after him—just as he knew who it would be. Jinx's wrangler.

The thought turned his stomach. Earlier, he'd had a nice drunk going. He'd felt cocky and self-assured. He'd outsmarted his so-smart wife. He'd had her in his clutches.

Now he was running scared. He could just hear his father telling him how he'd really screwed up his life good this time. He was looking at jail. Maybe even prison. Why hadn't he let it go? Why hadn't he let Jinx go? But he knew the answer. She was the best thing that had ever happened to him.

But following her up on this mountain? It had been as stupid as Travis had said. He blamed his pride. Everyone in the county knew that Jinx had kicked him out. What was he supposed to do? He couldn't stand looking like a beaten dog with his tail between his legs. He couldn't just let her get away with that.

Now as he stumbled through the pines feeling sick to his stomach and scared, he didn't want to be that man anymore. He wanted desperately to be different, but he had no idea how to make that happen. He felt as if he'd been forced into his bad behavior his whole life. First, by his father's taunts. Later, by the knowledge that he wasn't any good. He wasn't good enough, especially for Jinx. It was why he drank. The more he drank, the worse things got, but he hadn't been able to stop. He'd never been able to stop himself on any of it. For the life of him, he couldn't just let things alone.

Like now. He kept running instead of doing the smart thing and surrendering. He could hear a second helicopter coming. Why not just give up? He needed medical attention. He was still bleeding. He wasn't even sure he could get away. Why not make things easier for himself?

Because there was something in his DNA that wouldn't let him. *That and arrogance*, he thought. Then again, a part of him believed he could get away. He knew this mountain. He knew how to get off it to the closest ranch. He knew how to get help from someone who wouldn't call the cops. He could get away and save himself, and knowing that was what kept him going.

What he didn't know was how badly Jinx had been hit. He'd felt her drop to the ground when he'd released her. There'd been blood everywhere. He hadn't known if it was his or hers. Now he knew that at least part of it was his. But he was sure she'd been hit. Who had fired the shot, though? Not the wrangler. Maybe one of his buddies. Or maybe even Max. Max hated him, just as Jinx's father had.

He pushed those thoughts away as he ran, one surfacing that made him stumble and almost fall. What if Jinx was dead?

The thought hit him so hard that he had trouble staying on his feet. He loved her. His heart broke at the thought that she might be gone. He knew he'd said he was going to kill her—and he might have—but it wasn't what he'd wanted. He hadn't pulled the trigger. He wasn't sure he ever would have been able to.

He'd just had to let her know he wouldn't be simply sent away like some orphan child she was tired of having around. He thought of his mother who'd deserted him when he was nine. He remembered standing at the window, snot running from his nose as he cried and pleaded for her not to leave.

His father had found him and practically tore off his arm as he'd jerked him away from the window. "I'll beat you to within an inch of your life if you don't quit crying. She's gone. Accept it. I have. I never want to hear her name spoken in this house again. Now man up. You and me? We're on our own so make the best of it."

The memory still hurt. He had to stop for moment to catch his breath. Each breath was now a labor. What if the bullet had clipped one of his lungs? What if it was filling with blood right now?

T.D. knew he had to keep moving—even if it killed him. He took off again, holding his hand wrapped in his bandanna over his wound, aware that the bandanna was soaked with his blood.

Growing more light-headed, he felt as if he'd been running his whole life. He was a runner like his mother, he thought. She had gotten away. He feared he wouldn't be so lucky.

Chapter Sixteen

Angus stopped to look ahead in the pines. Had he lost T.D.? He glanced down and saw a drop of blood on the dried pine needles. He looked for another and saw it a few yards away. The blood drops were getting farther apart and smaller, which meant the man wasn't bleeding as badly as he'd been earlier. He would soon be harder to trail. He had to find him before that. He had to find him before he got away. T.D. knew this mountain. He would know how to escape—if he was able.

Angus stared into the shadows of the dense pines, looking for movement, listening for even the sound of a twig snapping. He heard nothing, saw nothing move. He knew T.D. wasn't armed. He knew that the man had dropped the gun he'd been holding to Jinx's head. Unless he had another weapon on him, he was at a distinct disadvantage that way.

However, T.D. had one very good advantage.

He was somewhere ahead, and he had enough of a head start that he could be lying in wait somewhere up there. Angus would be expecting an ambush, but would he get a chance to fire his pistol before T.D. sprung his own trap?

It was still a mystery as to who had shot T.D. and Jinx. The rifle report had echoed across the mountain. He'd thought it had come from behind him, but he couldn't be sure. The gunshot had startled them all—even T.D. Angus remembered the sound of a rider taking off not long after the second shot.

Now as he searched the ground for more blood, he worried about Jinx and his brother. He knew that Ella was with Brick, and Max with Jinx. Help had arrived and they both were getting treated for their injuries. Still, a part of him wanted to turn back even though he knew there was nothing he could do to help them.

This wasn't his job, going after T. D. Sharp. He told himself to let him go as he heard one of the helicopters lift off again. Let the sheriff handle this. Anyway, T.D. might already be bleeding to death up here on this mountain like the wild animal he was.

But Angus didn't turn back. He kept going, stubbornly, not willing to chance that the man might get away with what he'd done. Had T.D. heard the helicopters arrive and now begun to take off again? Would he head for them, choosing medical attention over freedom?

ELLA HELD BRICK'S hand in the helicopter on the way to the hospital. He was in and out of consciousness, but the EMTs had stopped the bleeding and were monitoring his vital signs. They weren't as strong as they would like, they'd said.

She kept thinking about how he hadn't wanted to come to Wyoming. How he'd wanted to go see that woman he liked up by the border. Had he sensed that coming here... She shoved the thought away, telling herself that none of them had known he would be shot. Even with all her intuitiveness, she hadn't known this was going to happen.

Brick opened his eyes. "Angus?" he whispered.

"He's fine," she said, even though she didn't know that for sure. As Jinx was being loaded into the second helicopter, Max had told Ella that Angus had gone after T.D., who'd been wounded. Max said Angus had saved Jinx's life. Then he had climbed in with her and the helicopter had taken off.

Just as Ella's chopper with Brick was about to take off, a man had come running out of the woods saying his arm was broken. The EMTs seemed to know him and called him by name— Travis. They'd let him climb in. Ella knew he was a friend of T.D.'s. He sat away from her, looking scared and avoiding eye contact as if he also knew he had more trouble than a broken arm.

Ella squeezed Brick's hand and prayed for him and Angus. It was just like him to go after T.D. Jinx had been hit but was going to make it, the EMTs had said. Angus had saved Jinx, according to Max. So why hadn't he waited and let the sheriff handle T.D.?

Because he was worried the man would get away and go after Jinx yet again, she thought. He was probably right.

JINX DIDN'T REMEMBER much of the helicopter ride to the hospital. Max had been there, telling her everything was going to be all right. She knew better than that.

Now she watched the nurse and doctor moving around the ER as she lay on a gurney in a daze. Max said Angus had saved her. She just remembered T.D., his arm around her neck, stars dancing before her eyes as he cut off her oxygen, and a gun to her temple. He'd said he was going to kill her, and she hadn't doubted that he would before Angus had appeared on the mountainside above them.

She'd thought at first that Angus had fired the shot. But she swore it had come from another direction. She'd felt the bullet graze her temple and hit T.D. He'd shuddered behind her, loosening his hold on her throat and then letting her go.

Close to blacking out, she'd dropped to her knees, gasping for breath. As Angus had rushed to her, she'd seen Wyatt Hanson in the trees. He was holding a rifle, the barrel pointed right at them and then, as if realizing he'd been seen, he'd taken off on his horse.

The rest was a blur except for Angus's handsome face above her, his look of concern in those blue eyes and then his smile when he realized she was going to be all right.

She'd looked down to see the blood, unsure how much of it was hers and how much of it was T.D.'s. And then Max was there, telling Angus to go after T.D. She'd wanted to stop him, but everything seemed to be happening too fast.

Now her heart ached with worry for Angus. He'd gone after T.D. and as far as she knew, no one had seen him since.

When the elderly doctor she'd known her whole life came into her ER room, she asked him if anyone else had been admitted. He shook his head as he checked her pulse. "Angus Savage?"

"Brick Savage is on his way to surgery. I don't believe Angus Savage has been brought in."

"T. D. Sharp?" she asked.

The doctor shook his head. "The sheriff is here, though. Are you up to answering a few questions?"

She nodded. She kept remembering being shot up on the mountain and Max saying, "The helicopters are here. They're setting down in the meadow now. It's going to be all right."

But Jinx had known that nothing was going to be all right. Angus was still up in the mountains chasing T.D. and she was here. She mouthed a silent prayer for both Brick and Angus.

The sheriff was beside her bed, holding her hand, and she was crying hard. "It's all my fault," she kept saying in between her racking sobs. "All my fault."

Harvey tried to tell her that it wasn't, that he had to check on the others and would be back.

As he started to leave, she grabbed his hand again. "T.D. is still up there. Angus Savage went after him. You have to find them."

"We will," he promised.

"Please don't let anything happen to Angus."

The sheriff smiled and squeezed her hand. "Don't worry."

But all she could do was worry, head pounding. She thought of that young cowboy whom she'd shoved out that barn loft window. She'd almost gotten him killed that day on the Cardwell Ranch when they were little more than kids and here she was again jeopardizing his life. She thought of Angus, his handsome face glowing in the campfire light. The man was like granite, solid and strong.

She clung to that. She had to believe that no matter what happened up on the mountain, Angus would survive. He had to, she thought, her heart aching.

ANGUS MOVED CAUTIOUSLY through the pines, scanning the terrain ahead for movement. He'd seen the red marks on Jinx's throat along with the tiny specks of blood splattered there so he'd known what had happened, even if he hadn't seen T.D. holding her in a headlock, a pistol to her head.

What he didn't know is who had taken such a dangerous shot. Jinx could have been killed. As it was, the bullet had only grazed her temple. But just one wrong move by her or her shooter…

But that hadn't happened, he reminded himself, pushing away the image that lodged in his brain. Instead, Jinx had gotten lucky. She was alive. T.D. had taken the bullet and once Angus found the man, he'd put an end to this.

That was if T.D. was still alive. His hope was that he would come upon the man's body lying in the dried pine needles. He didn't want to kill him, but he would if it came to that.

Ahead, he saw movement and quickly stepped behind a tree. He could hear something busting through the underbrush on the side of the mountain. He frowned. Too large for a man? He peered around the tree in time to see several moose that had been spooked out of their beds. He glanced in the direction they'd come from, knowing that was where he would find T.D.

Chapter Seventeen

Wyatt couldn't stop shaking. The ride down the mountain had been at breakneck speed. He'd practically killed his horse and himself. But all he'd been able to think of was getting to Patty. He didn't want anyone else telling her what had happened.

He'd heard the helicopters but had stayed in the trees hoping no one saw him. Not that it would make any difference. There was always the chance that the sheriff could tell which rifle had fired the shot. That was why the only stop he'd made was to drop his rifle into an old mill shaft at the edge of the mountain. He'd thrown in a bunch of rocks to cover it, before getting back on his horse and riding the rest of the way to the corral where he kept his horse.

Wyatt knew there was no way to cover the fact that he'd been up on that mountain. Too many people knew he'd been there. Even if he said that he'd left before they'd gone up to Jinx's camp, there was one person in particular who knew better. The person who'd seen him after he'd fired the first rifle shot. T.D. T.D. knew that he'd shot him. T.D. probably even knew that he'd fired a second shot, trying to finish him off.

That thought rattled him clear to the toes of his boots. He told himself it had been an accident. That he'd been trying to kill Jinx. Or had he, at the last minute, lifted the rifle just a little? Had he seen T.D. in the crosshairs of his scope? Had he realized Patty would never be free as long as T. D. Sharp was alive? Is that what made him take the shot? Or had it really been an accident, his arms fatigued from holding the rifle up for so long, his finger on the trigger jittery at even the thought of what he was about to do?

It was a short walk from the corral to Patty's. He stumbled up to her door after leaving his horse at a ranch on the edge of town. As he tried to catch his breath and still the trembling inside him, he knocked, then knocked louder. He couldn't help looking around as if any minute he expected to hear sirens and turn to find a SWAT team with their weapons trained on him.

The door finally opened. "I shot them." Wyatt pushed his way into her apartment, practically falling in, his legs were so weak.

"Them?" Patty said.

He realized he hadn't meant to say that. But he had. "I shot Jinx. And T.D."

"You *what*?" Patty cried. "Is T.D....dead?"

"I don't know. I didn't mean to. It was an accident. I swear. I was doing what you asked me to. T.D. had Jinx by the throat. She was struggling..."

"Is Jinx dead?"

"I don't know. It all happened so fast." He rushed into the living room and dropped onto the couch. "She was on the ground. There was so much blood. And then I saw T.D. He was holding his chest and there was blood everywhere. That's when I hightailed it off that mountain. It was horrible."

Wyatt dropped his face into his hands and broke down in tears.

"Tell me what happened," Patty said, her voice cracking. When he didn't respond, she came over to the couch and sat down beside him to shake his shoulder. *"Tell me what happened."*

He took a gulp of air and tried to still his sobs. This was not the way he'd wanted Patty to see him. But he couldn't help himself. He was terrified of what he'd done and the price he would be forced to pay.

"Wyatt," she said as if talking to a child. "Pull yourself together and tell me what happened."

He nodded. After a moment he stopped crying, wiped his face with his sleeve and swallowed as he saw that all the color had left her face. She now stared at him as if in shock.

Wyatt cleared his voice and began. "T.D. said we were going to stampede the cattle, but they were waiting for us. They'd set up these booby traps and I heard Travis get caught in one. I think Cash and Royce did, too." His voice cracked. "I think they might be dead." He started to put his face back into his hands, but Patty grabbed one hand and, shaking her head, said, "Tell me how T.D. got shot."

"He never planned to go with the others," Wyatt said. "He sent them in the way he figured Jinx would be expecting the attack. He and I went in the back way. T.D. double-crossed the men with him. He had no intention of stampeding the cattle. He was only after Jinx. Patty, he would never have stopped going after her. *Never.*"

PATTY STARED AT the man, wanting to scream at him, but her throat had gone dust dry. She was shaking inside, afraid she knew what the fool had done. Her worst fears had been realized. What had she been thinking asking Wyatt, of all people, to take care of this for her?

"You fired the shot?" she asked, trying hard to keep her voice level.

"I told you. It was an accident. I was trying to hit Jinx."

"You did hit her, right?" He nodded, looking down as if unable to meet her gaze. "And T.D.? You wouldn't have meant to shoot him. He's your best friend."

His head came up, his eyes full of tears and he nodded quickly. "T.D. had Jinx in a headlock with his pistol to her head. They must have moved when I fired."

"But you don't know how badly either of them was hit, right?"

He shook his head. "I panicked. I just had to get out of there."

He'd killed both Jinx *and* T.D.? Her hand itched to slap him until he quit his stupid blubbering. But she knew she was partially to blame for this. She'd known the man wasn't strong.

She hadn't expected him to do something so stupid as to kill T.D. Not T.D. She fought her own tears at the thought of him being gone. For so long, she dreamed of the day that she and T.D. would be husband and wife. They'd have kids, buy a house, maybe take a trip to Disney World.

That dream burst like a soap bubble. Even if T.D. wasn't dead, he might be lost to her.

"You're a good shot, aren't you?" she asked. "I mean, you beat T.D. and Travis every time at the state fair. You always get your elk and deer every year, killing them in one shot, not spoiling any meat. Isn't that right, Wyatt?"

He nodded, but couldn't hold her gaze. She felt her heart drop. What had the man done?

Patty placed her hand on his thigh. He sniffed but was no longer crying. He wiped his face on his sleeve again and looked over at her as if the sun rose and set on her. "You say T.D. went after Jinx?"

He nodded and she listened as he told her how T.D. had been drinking and getting more angry every hour. The herd was almost to the summer grazing range. They were running out of time.

"You know how he gets when he drinks," Wyatt said, his voice hoarse. "He was crazy. There was no talking him out of it." She patted his thigh and told him to continue. "He and I went in through the camp, but then he found Jinx and started dragging her down the mountain away from the others.

"Travis got hurt first. I heard him scream. Through the trees I could see that he'd been knocked off his horse. I heard him say his arm was broken. Then I think Cash and Royce got caught. That's when I heard a gunshot, then another. I didn't know what was going on. I don't know who all were killed."

"Because you were following T.D. so you could get a good shot at Jinx," she reminded him.

He nodded and swallowed, looking guilty. "I

was watching them through the scope on my rifle." He met her gaze. "I was just doing what you asked me to."

Patty removed her hand from his thigh. She could see that was exactly what he would tell the sheriff. That she'd made a deal with him to kill Jinx. She had no doubt that under pressure, he would break down. He would tell the sheriff that it had been her idea. Knowing Wyatt, the fool would probably even tell the sheriff what she'd promised him if he killed Jinx for her. She could deny it, but she feared that Wyatt would be the more believable one, especially if it went to trial.

Panic rose in her, but she tamped it back down. If T.D. was dead, what did she care if she went to prison? Her life would be over without him. But maybe he wasn't. Maybe all of this could be saved.

She tried to think. "Where is everyone now?" Wyatt was sobbing again into his hands. She shook his shoulder again. "Where is everyone now?"

He lifted his head, wiping his face with his sodden sleeve as he tried to pull himself together again. "I saw helicopters. Two of them. The medical ones. I guess the injured are at the hospital by now. I had to get out of there before they saw me."

So whoever had survived this fiasco had gone to the hospital—or was still up on the mountain. "You should stay here," she said. Wyatt brightened. "I'll go to the hospital and find out who all made it." He nodded, looking miserable again. "I'll be back. You should get some rest. Whatever you do, don't leave, okay?" He nodded. "Don't talk to anyone. I mean *anyone*. This is just between the two of us." He nodded again, looking hopeful.

She told herself that if she played this right, she might be able to save herself. If not, it would be her word against Wyatt's. She didn't even have to guess which the sheriff would believe since he'd known them both since they were kids. Which meant she was going to have to get Wyatt to lie. With a sigh, she knew what she'd have to do in that case.

Patty dressed quickly. If T.D. was alive, then he could be one of those brought out by helicopter. She imagined him in the hospital, injured, but alive. She refused to even consider that he was dead up there on the mountain along with all of her dreams.

T.D. was strong and smart and determined, she assured herself. He would survive—he had to. Once she saw him, she'd have to deal with Wyatt. That prospect had little appeal. If only he'd done what she'd asked. He'd said he'd seen Jinx on the ground. He'd said he'd seen blood. Maybe the shot he'd taken had passed through her and hit T.D., barely wounding him. That was possible.

She hung on to the hope that Jinx was dead and

T.D. merely injured. Still, she wanted to throttle Wyatt. The damned fool. Why would he take a shot when T.D. was struggling with Jinx?

Because she'd asked him to kill Jinx.

Unfortunately, she feared that wasn't all that was going through Wyatt's mind during that instant when he'd pulled that trigger. The man was too good a shot to do something so stupid. So reckless. So dangerous. But if she was right, then that, too, would be her fault.

Her blood ran cold at what she might have done—signed T.D.'s death warrant. But maybe it wasn't too late. Maybe T.D. was still alive. Maybe it wasn't too late for her, either. Maybe she could cover her tracks.

Then there was Wyatt. Would the sheriff be looking for him? Not yet. She had time.

She drove to the hospital on the edge of town, trying to remain calm. But the moment she pushed in through the emergency entrance, she saw people scurrying around and felt her skin turn clammy. Spotting a young blond-haired, green-eyed woman in soiled Western attire, she stepped to her.

"Were you with the McCallahan Ranch cattle drive?" she asked.

The woman nodded.

"Can you tell me who was brought into the hospital?"

Just then the sheriff walked out of one of the ER rooms. He headed straight for her.

"Thought I might find you here, Patty." Sheriff Bessler was looking at her as if all of this was her fault.

She bristled under his gaze, but held her temper. There was only one thing she wanted to know. "Is T.D....?"

"I don't know any more than you do at this point except that your boyfriend had no business up there and now I've got two gunshot victims." He pushed past her. "Go home, Patty," he said over his shoulder. "If your boy is alive, he's going to jail."

"What about Jinx?" she asked, making the big man stop in his tracks and turn back to her.

"No thanks to T.D. she's going to be fine," the sheriff said, his face set in stone. "She was treated and released. If you see T.D., Patty, you call me or I'll slap you with assisting and abetting a wanted man. You don't think I will? Try me." With that he turned and walked away.

Patty couldn't believe the injustice. Jinx was fine. But T.D. was wounded somewhere up on that mountain? She turned around and saw the young woman wrangler. "Please, you were up there with them. Can you tell me if T.D. is okay?" she asked, hating the panic in her voice.

ELLA CONSIDERED THE woman the sheriff had called Patty. From what she'd gathered, this was T. D. Sharp's girlfriend. Right now all she could think about was Brick and Angus. Brick was up in surgery. She had no idea where Angus was or if he was still alive.

But she couldn't ignore the pain in the woman's voice. "I don't know. I heard he was wounded. That's all I can tell you." Patty started to turn away. "What I do know is that because of T.D., my cousin is fighting for his life and his brother could be, as well, up on that mountain. He'd gone after your boyfriend."

"But T.D. was alive?"

Ella heard no compassion in the woman's voice for the people T.D. had hurt and had to turn away, her sympathy for the woman waning. She walked back down the hall to wait, too worried about both of her cousins to deal with T.D.'s lover.

She told herself that both Brick and Angus were strong. They were fighters. Which meant that Angus wouldn't give up until he found T.D. and finished this. Her heart ached at the thought. T.D. could kill him up there on the mountain and they might never find him.

While she tried to concentrate on thinking positive, she was exhausted. Her senses seemed dulled down to nothing but static. Worry made her heart ache. She told herself they would both be fine, but she didn't feel it in her soul and that terrified her.

Dropping into a chair in the hallway outside the ER rooms, she closed her eyes and prayed. She thought of Brick in surgery. In the helicopter, he'd come to long enough to tell her what had happened on the mountain—how Royce had shot him after Brick had captured him and bound his wrists. Either he or Cash had had a second gun that he'd missed.

The EMTs tried to get Brick not to talk, but he seemed determined to get the words out. "I killed him. I didn't even hesitate after he shot me. I just pulled the trigger." Brick had closed his eyes. "I killed him."

"Only in self-defense," she'd assured him.

She'd heard the anguish in his words as he repeated them. *"I killed a man."*

And then the alarms had gone off and the EMTs were fighting to save Brick's life as the helicopter set down next to the hospital and he was rushed to surgery.

She said another prayer for him, terrified that she would lose both of her cousins. *Please, let them be all right.* Ella needed both men in her life. She couldn't do without either of them. And she didn't even want to imagine what Dana would do if she lost her boys.

Chapter Eighteen

Back home, Jinx felt as if she was going crazy with worry about Angus and Brick and now Max. Earlier when the doctor finally came back in her room before releasing her, she'd said, "I know you said I have a mild concussion so that could be the problem, but I swear I haven't seen Max since I was brought in."

Dr. Kirkland had nodded solemnly, making her heart drop. "I've admitted him. Now, don't get excited," he'd said quickly before she could panic. "He was having some chest pain. Nothing to worry about, but I wanted to keep him overnight for observation. I want to do the same with you."

"I want to see him," she'd said and started to get up off the gurney, but he'd laid a hand on her arm and shaken his head.

"Max is resting. Seeing your concern will only agitate him. I've assured him that you are fine. Now I've assured you that he is fine. Both of you just need rest. You've been through a lot. You can see Max tomorrow. Now please stop fighting me."

She'd lain back but was too restless to stay there. Sitting up again, she'd said, "Please let me go home. I'm going crazy here. And you know I'll sneak up and check on Max if I'm forced to stay here overnight."

Dr. Kirkland had chuckled and given her a look of disbelief. But he'd known her long enough—since the night he delivered her—that he knew her well. "I'd like you to stay, but your concussion is very mild. I see nothing in your vitals to be concerned about. The bullet wound will heal, but you'll have a scar."

She'd thought of Angus's scar—the one she'd basically given him. "I don't mind." It was the scars you couldn't see that bothered her.

The doctor had studied her. "I suspect you have a terrific headache, am I right?"

"It's not bad," she'd lied. "Please, Doc. I'd feel better at home." But she'd known she wouldn't feel better until Angus was found alive and safe and Max was back at the ranch. "Is there any word on Brick Savage yet?"

"He's still in surgery. He had a really close call. Surely there are even more things you need to worry about." He had no idea—or maybe he did.

Dr. Kirkland had finally agreed to discharge

her if she promised to take it easy at home. He'd said he'd see to the paperwork.

"I'd feel better if she stayed here," the sheriff had said as he pushed aside the curtain in her ER room.

"You two work it out," Dr. Kirkland had said as he left.

"Have you heard anything?" she'd asked Harvey.

He'd shaken his head. "Since you feel good enough to go home, I'm sure you're up to some questions."

"Shouldn't you be up on the mountain looking for Angus?"

"I have deputies up there right now searching for both Angus and T.D. Anyone else I should be looking for?"

"Cash and Royce were up there. Wyatt and Travis."

The sheriff had nodded. "Travis is getting his arm cast as we speak and from what I heard, Royce is dead. A chopper will be taking me up to the mountain soon, so why don't you tell me what happened. I've already gotten the story from others who were brought in, except for Brick. He's still in surgery."

She had given him a shortened version. When she finished, he asked, "Booby traps?" and shook his head. "You say you don't know who shot you and T.D.?"

"No, but I saw Wyatt Hanson with a rifle and he rode away right after the shooting stopped."

The sheriff had mumbled something under his breath. All she caught was "wouldn't blame one of his own for taking a potshot at him," before he said, "What the hell was T.D. thinking, going up there after you?"

"Like I know what makes him do what he does. As I told you, he started a grass fire, trying to stampede my herd, but we got that put out. We knew he'd hit again so we made some booby traps to slow them down."

His gaze had saddened. "He tried to rape you."

"But he didn't. Angus stopped him and so did whoever shot him."

Still, the sheriff had looked distraught. "I wish I could have been able to stop him from going up there. Unfortunately, there is no law against riding up into the mountains. But you could have called when you saw him. Even if I hadn't been able to arrest him..."

"What would you have done? We had no proof that T.D. had started the fire. He hadn't gotten anyone killed at that point. He hadn't even gotten close enough to me to arrest him for breaking the restraining order."

"Fortunately, Ella Cardwell climbed a tree on top of the mountain and was able to reach 911 for help. Smart woman."

Jinx had mugged a face at him. "What do you want me to say? That I should have sold my cattle at a loss and never gone up on that mountain?" She'd felt a sob climb her throat. "I wish I had."

The sheriff had laid a hand on hers. "None of this is your fault. This all falls on T.D. and those fools he got to go along with him." Harvey's radio had gone off. He'd checked it and said, "I have to go. They have a helicopter ready to take me up there. Anything else I should know?"

"Just find Angus, please."

"And T.D.," he'd added pointedly. "Until he's behind bars, you won't be safe. Which is another reason I'd like you to stay here tonight."

She'd shaken her head. "He's up on that mountain somewhere wounded. I'm not worried about him. You're going to find him anyway and lock him up." She'd smiled at the sheriff. "I'll be at the house. I have my shotgun loaded by the door."

"Great. We love it when private citizens take the law into their own hands. Nothing can go wrong with that."

"If he so much as steps on my porch, I'm going to shoot him," she'd said with a fierceness that she could see even surprised the sheriff. "He is never touching me again."

The sheriff had looked at her for a long moment before he'd drawn her to him and hugged her. "I'd send a deputy out to your house but—"

"You need them up on the mountain to find Angus and T.D. I'll be fine."

He hadn't looked convinced of that. "I'll call as soon as I know something."

"Promise?"

"Promise."

ANGUS COULD SEE a rock rim ahead. He slowed, feeling the air around him seem to still. The sun was golden against a blue sky studded with puffy white clouds. The morning was cold and crisp and completely still now that the helicopters had left.

But he knew that the sheriff could be arriving soon to search for T.D., pick up Royce's body and investigate the crime scene. The cattle had scattered with the landing of the urgent care helicopters. It was just one more thing Jinx would have to worry about. Angus was determined that T.D. wouldn't still be on that list.

The silence on the mountain took on an eerie feel that made the hair on the back of his neck prickle. He felt as if he and T.D. were the only ones left on the planet. He figured they were the only ones still alive left on this mountain.

Angus studied the terrain ahead of him. He saw no movement, heard nothing for a long moment. A squirrel began to chatter at him from a nearby tree. A jet left a contrail in the sky overhead.

He knew he should turn back and wait for the sheriff. This wasn't his job. But all his instincts told him that he was close and that if he didn't stop T.D., he would get away. Even if he didn't go after Jinx right away, he would always be a threat to her. She would have to be on constant guard, waiting for the other shoe to drop, waiting for him to suddenly appear. When he did...

Angus knew that was why he had to find T.D. and end this. His pistol ready, he moved into the pines beneath the rock rim, knowing that if T.D. was going to hide somewhere, the rocks under the rim would be the perfect place.

He'd expected an ambush. He'd expected gunfire when he got close enough. T.D. had dropped his pistol, but that didn't mean he didn't have another weapon. Angus hadn't seen any blood on the ground for a while now. T.D. wasn't mortally wounded. That meant he was even more dangerous since even if he wasn't armed, he could launch himself from a tree or a rock. T.D. would have the element of surprise.

Angus reached an open area and stopped beside a tree. A slight breeze moaned in the tops of the tall pines. He listened for a closer sound. Movement through the grass as someone approached. The snap of a twig under a boot heel. A stumble overturning a rock.

Hearing nothing, he spotted an object caught

on the tall grass in the middle of the clearing. It appeared to be a blood-soaked bandanna.

Angus moved toward it, watching the tree line ahead as he did. When the warning came it was too late. He heard a rumble like thunder and looked up the mountainside. The rocks T.D. had dislodged were bounding down the steep slope directly toward him. The man had left the bandanna on the tall grass knowing Angus would see it and believe he'd crossed the clearing. T.D. had known he was following his blood trail.

The ruse had worked. Angus had only a few seconds to decide which way to run—forward or try to double back. The rocks had dislodged other rocks and started a landslide that filled the clearing above him.

Angus realized belatedly that the clearing was an old avalanche chute. There was nothing to stop the landslide now barreling down the mountainside toward him.

In those few seconds he had, he made up his mind. He sprinted forward, hoping to get to the trees before the landslide caught him up in it.

The damp, dew-soaked new grass was slick, his cowboy boots slipping and losing purchase. Once, he almost fell when his feet threatened to slide out from under him. He ran as hard and fast as he could. His legs ached from the sudden intensity of his effort. His lungs burned. He could hear the low rumble getting louder and louder, so close he could feel the air it displaced as it roared down the mountainside.

He was almost to the trees. Just a few more yards. A large rock appeared in front of him, careening past. Then another. He tried to dodge the next one. It clipped him in the leg, knocking him to the ground.

He rolled, the shelter of the trees so close he could almost reach it. A rock hit him in the side, knocking the breath out of him as he pulled himself up on all fours and launched himself into the trees. A fist-size rock bounced just as he threw himself forward. It smacked him in the head.

The lights went out before he hit the ground.

Chapter Nineteen

T.D. stared down the mountainside. He'd seen the wrangler get hit a couple of times by the rocks tumbling down the slope. Now all he could make out was the cowboy's boots, still visible, protruding from one of the pines along the side of the clearing.

Was the man dead? Pretending to be dead? T.D. pressed his glove over his wound. He'd gotten it bleeding worse with the effort of pushing off the rocks to get the landslide started. But it had worked. The cowboy still hadn't gotten up.

He waited, unsure what to do. Go down and check to make sure the man wouldn't be after him again? Take the man's gun and finish him? Or just get the hell out of Dodge?

He felt light-headed from loss of blood. He knew he needed a doctor. Fortunately, there was someone who was fairly close to a doctor who could patch him up and would without calling the sheriff. All he had to do was get off this mountain. He was pretty sure the bullet had gone clean through his chest just below his left shoulder. With luck, he would live.

The wrangler still hadn't moved. He knew he probably couldn't trust his thinking since he suspected he might be in shock. He wouldn't have minded finishing the bastard off. The cowboy had come to Jinx's rescue not once, but again last night. He'd seen them together. He knew that look of Jinx's.

Just the thought made his blood boil. The sound of another helicopter made up his mind for him. He took one last look at the cowboy still lying at the edge of the pines unmoving and then he turned toward the game trail that he knew would lead him off this mountain to a ranch where he could get the help he needed.

He hadn't gone far when he saw a saddled horse standing in the middle of the trail. He recognized the mount as Royce's and couldn't believe his luck. The mount was dragging its reins as if it had gotten spooked and come untied. He wondered where Royce was, but the thought was a quickly passing one.

T. D. Sharp wasn't going to look a gift horse in the mouth, so to speak.

JINX WILLED HER phone to ring. The sheriff had promised he would call her the moment he knew anything about Angus Savage as well as T.D.

She knew Harvey would do as he promised. Which meant he hadn't found Angus or T.D. Just the thought of all that country up on that mountain... The men could be anywhere. T.D. was wounded, but that didn't mean that he couldn't be dangerous. Angus had come all this way to help her and now he could be dead.

She found herself pacing the floor even though the doctor had told her to take it easy. She said she would or he wouldn't have released her from the hospital. Her temple felt tender under the bandage and her head ached. She'd been going crazy at the hospital. She hated feeling like an invalid on an emergency room gurney when she hadn't been injured that badly. Worse, she hated feeling helpless.

The sheriff was right. She liked to believe she could take care of herself. She'd never liked asking for help, especially after she'd kicked T.D. out. She'd wanted to show everyone that she could handle all of this—the ranch, her father's death, T.D. and the divorce.

But as strong as she knew she was, she'd needed help. She didn't know what she would have done without Angus, Brick, Ella and Max. Her eyes filled with tears. Her stubbornness had put them all in jeopardy.

Picking up her phone, she called the hospital to check on Max and Brick.

"Both are sleeping comfortably, Jinx," the nurse she knew told her. "Ella Cardwell is on a cot in her cousin's room. Everyone is down for the night. Just like you should be."

She knew the nurse was right as she touched the bandage on her temple. Her head still ached, but it had dulled. She hung up, thinking of the scar she would have, which made her think of Angus's small one on his chin. She wished she were in his arms right now. She closed her eyes as she remembered the heat of their kisses. Stolen kisses and one of the few things she would never regret.

You're falling for him. Her eyes flew open. No. True or not, she couldn't trust her heart. Not now. Not with the divorce and knowing she was losing the ranch. Anyway, how could she possibly trust something that had happened so quickly? She couldn't. She'd leaned on Angus. He'd come to her rescue. He'd saved her life.

Of course she felt something for him. But love? She shook her head even as her heart drummed in her chest at the thought of the man, and worry nagged at her. He had to be all right. He just had to. She couldn't bear the thought that T.D. might kill him. That she might never see Angus alive again. Her heart ached with worry.

Why hadn't the sheriff called? Hours had gone by. Maybe he hadn't found either Angus or T.D.

Or maybe he'd found them both. She knew Harvey. He'd never tell someone over the phone about a death of a loved one. That was something he did, hat in hand, head bowed, at the person's door.

Chapter Twenty

Angus surfaced to the sound of a helicopter. He opened his eyes. How long had he been out? Not that long, he told himself as he found the sun still glowing in Wyoming's big sky. But he had lost some time.

He tried to sit up, his head swimming. He gingerly touched the spot where the last rock had clocked him. It was painful. He looked around, blinked. T.D. Where was the man? Turning carefully, he glanced back up the mountain. Why hadn't the man taken advantage when he was out cold and finished him? Because T.D. wasn't really a killer? Or because he wanted to get off this mountain as fast as he could?

Pushing himself to his feet, he glanced down the mountain to where the helicopter was hovering before setting down. He headed in that direction although he felt dizzy, his head aching and his footsteps unsure. When he heard the rotors on the helicopter finally stop, he pulled his pistol and fired three shots into the air.

His call for help was answered by a returned three reports, one after the other. He holstered his gun and kept walking in the direction of the chopper. By now, this mountain had to be crawling with cops. Was it possible they'd caught T.D.? He couldn't bear to think the man had gotten away.

Ahead, he could make out the helicopter through the trees. It had landed in a clearing. Before he could reach it, a deputy sheriff intercepted him, demanding to know who he was.

"Angus Cardwell Savage," he said, feeling light-headed.

"Mr. Savage, are you aware that you're bleeding?"

He never got to answer because he'd seen the sheriff coming through the pines toward him and then darkness closed in again.

PATTY KNEW SHE should go home, but Wyatt was there and she wasn't ready to deal with him yet. She pushed into the bar and headed for a stool. It was early enough in the afternoon that the place was almost empty. Just the way she liked it when she was feeling the way she was.

Marty came down the bar. He looked surprised to see her. She still felt bad about what she'd said to him before. "Cola?"

She shook her head. "Whiskey. Straight up." Her voice broke and she was glad when he merely nodded and went down the bar to get her drink. She was in no mood for small talk, let alone anything deeper. She didn't need to be told again what everyone thought about her and T.D.

Just the thought of T.D. brought tears to her eyes. He couldn't be dead. Wouldn't she know it in her heart if he was? And what was she going to do about Wyatt?

Marty set a shot glass full of whiskey on a napkin in front of her and put down the bottle next to it. "Thought I'd save myself the walk back," he said.

She could tell he was waiting—just in case she wanted to talk. She picked up the shot glass and threw back the whiskey. It burned all the way down. Her eyes watered again, this time from the alcohol. "I'm sorry about—"

He waved that off. "Bartenders are just supposed to listen. No one with a lick of sense would take advice from one." He started to turn back down the bar.

"Marty," she said and reached out to touch his forearm to stop him. "I don't want to be me," she said as she removed her hand from his arm. "I hate the person I've become but I don't know how to change."

"Everyone has days like that."

"No, not like this one," she said and poured herself another shot. For a moment she merely stared at the warm golden liquid. "I'm going to have to do something I'm going to regret and yet, I don't have a choice, you know?"

Clearly, he didn't. He studied her openly. "Don't take this wrong but maybe you want to do whatever it is sober."

She laughed. "Not a chance." And threw down another shot.

JINX HAD THOUGHT she would feel better at home instead of in the hospital, but she'd been wrong. She found herself walking through the house as if lost as she kept reliving what had happened on the mountain.

She touched her throat, shuddering at the memory of T.D.'s arm locked around it. He'd cut off her air supply to the point that she'd almost blacked out. When she saw Angus appear, she'd thought she was dreaming. She'd seen the gun in his hand but thought he'd put it down. Had he fired the shot that had hit her and T.D.?

She still felt confused. Where had the shot come from? All she remembered was feeling something hit her in the head. T.D. had jerked, his arm loosening on her throat, as he stumbled back. She'd dropped to the ground, weak from lack of oxygen, blood dripping in her eyes. Hadn't there been another shot? She recalled turning to see T.D. holding a spot high on his chest.

He had looked confused as if like her, he hadn't known where the shots had come from. Then his expression had changed as if he saw something... someone in the distance. She'd followed his gaze and seen Wyatt holding a rifle and looking in their direction before jumping on his horse and taking off.

Wyatt had to have been the one who'd fired the shot—just as she'd told the sheriff. And yet, it made no sense. He was T.D.'s best friend, often his only friend. She frowned. Things had gotten so crazy up on that mountain, they might never be able to sort it out.

She just remembered that after she was shot, everything had happened so fast. It now felt like a blur. Angus she recalled had thrown his body over hers to protect her from further gunfire, flattening them both against the ground before Max had appeared and told Angus to go after T.D.

She could understand why both men wanted T.D. stopped. Hadn't she told the sheriff that she would kill him the next time he showed up here at the ranch? But all this waiting, all this worrying.

She pulled out her cell phone and called the sheriff to see if there had been any word. It went straight to voice mail. She reminded herself that Harvey had promised to call the moment he heard anything. He'd always been good to his word. He would call.

Or he'd show up at her door, she thought with a stab to her heart.

Walking to the window, she looked out. It was dark outside. She blinked in surprise. Exhaustion pulled at her. She knew she needed sleep because she couldn't account for the missing hours. Had she been pacing the floor all this time?

As she started to turn from the window, she heard the wind howling along the eaves. One of the fir trees scraped against the outside of the house as the others bent and swayed against a darkening sky. Another thunderstorm?

Jinx hugged herself, suddenly chilled. T.D. was still out there. For all she knew he was dead. But then again, she knew the man. He could be determined to the point of obsession when it was something he wanted.

If he could, he would survive and when he did, he would come after her.

Jinx shivered, hugging herself as she looked out into the darkness. Was Angus still up on the mountain? Why hadn't she heard anything? Just the thought of him made her heart ache. He'd gone after T.D. because he'd known—just as she had—that T.D. wouldn't stop. Not until she was dead.

She assured herself that by now half the county

had gone up into the mountains looking for T.D. They'd find him. They'd find Angus. Angus would be all right. They would find T.D. alive. He would be arrested. This would end and when it did...

That was the part, though, that she didn't have figured out yet. But she wasn't going to get it figured out tonight. Her head ached and she felt weak and sick with worry.

She'd never felt more alone. She kept remembering that her stubbornness had causes this mess. If she'd just sold the cattle, taking a loss, and given the money to T.D.... She knew that wouldn't have been enough for him. He wanted more than money. He wanted vengeance.

But at least she might be divorced from him by now. No longer his wife. No longer his. As long as they were husband and wife, he thought he could do anything he wanted with her. Right now she would gladly give him the ranch just to get him out of her life.

Just to know that Angus was all right.

Had Angus found T.D.? She knew T.D. would never fight fair. What if he'd seen Angus tracking him? What if he'd waited in ambush and killed him?

She turned away from the window, telling herself she had to have faith that Angus was all right. She had to because he'd made her want to go on when she'd felt like quitting, not just ranching, but life.

Max was getting too old for this. She knew that he wouldn't quit as long as she needed him. She thought about calling the hospital again, but knew she'd get the same report. She needed rest. If she could escape for even a little while in sleep…

Her cell phone rang, making her jump. She saw it was the sheriff and quickly picked up.

"Angus was found," he said quickly. "He's going to be fine. He was admitted to the hospital and no, you can't see him tonight. He has a concussion. Was hit in the head, but as I said, Doc assured me that he will be fine."

She felt a flood of relief that brought tears to her eyes. "And T.D.?"

Harvey was silent for a moment. "He got away. That's why I'm sending a deputy out to your place as soon as the shifts change. Most everyone has been up on the mountain looking for him."

"You don't need to send a deputy out here."

"Don't tell me how to do my job, young lady. I'm worried about you. The deputy will just sit outside your house. He won't bother you."

"You sound tired," she said, touched by Harvey's concern for her.

"I am. You sound tired yourself. I thought the doctor said you could go home but only if you rested."

She smiled to herself. "I was just heading to bed. Thank you for letting me know."

"Sleep well."

"You, too." She hung up and headed for her bedroom. Now that she knew Angus was all right, she might be able to get some sleep, she thought as she turned out the lights as she went.

She'd reached her bedroom door and fumbled in the pitch-black room to flip the light switch. Nothing happened. *The overhead lightbulb must have gone out*, she thought. She was working toward her nightstand next to the bed to turn on that lamp when she heard a sound that stopped her cold.

Someone was in the room. In the room waiting for her in the dark. Her blood turned to slush as she said, "Who's there?" fearing she already knew.

Chapter Twenty-One

Jinx let her hand drop to the nightstand drawer. "I know you're there," she said as she eased it open and felt around for the pistol.

It was gone.

The lamp on the nightstand across the bed snapped on, illuminating Patty Conroe sitting in the chair beside the bed. She was holding the pistol from Jinx's bedside table.

"Patty?" She felt confused to see the woman for a moment. She'd been expecting T.D. But as she looked at her husband's lover, she knew she should have been anticipating this visit for some time. "What do you want?"

"What you've taken from me," Patty said.

"What I've taken from *you*?"

Patty's once pretty face showed the road map her life had taken since the two of them were in high school together. "T.D. was mine first."

"You can have him." She noticed the way the

woman was holding the gun. Patty knew how to use it.

"How's your head?" Patty asked offhandedly.

"Not fatal."

"That's too bad."

"Patty, where did you leave your car? I didn't see it when I came home."

"I left it behind that old barn on the way in so you wouldn't see it. I wanted to be here waiting for you the moment I heard you were being released from the hospital. The nurse was so helpful when I called."

"How did you get in here? I know the door was locked."

"I used T.D.'s key. You need to know the truth," the woman snapped. "T.D. came to me when he wasn't getting what he needed from you. I didn't lure him away from you."

"It doesn't matter," Jinx said with a sigh. "I'm divorcing him. He's going to be all yours."

"If he's not dead because of you." Patty sniffed, the pistol wavering in her hand.

Jinx smelled alcohol. She should have known that Patty wouldn't have come out here unless she had been intoxicated. In that way, she was a lot like T.D. And that made her more dangerous. "He's not dead."

"You can't know that," she cried.

She heard such heartbreak in the woman's

voice. Had she ever cared that much about T.D.? Not even when she'd married him. She hadn't known then what it felt like to really be in love with anyone, she realized. Her own heart was breaking at the thought of Angus injured and at the hospital because of her.

"Patty, put the gun down and go home. Your fight isn't with me."

The woman let out a bark of a laugh. "Are you serious? T.D. wouldn't be wounded and up on that mountain, possibly dead, if it wasn't for you," she said, her voice hoarse with emotion.

Jinx thought at least that might be true. "He's the one who followed me up there. You blame me for that?"

"You made him crazy. You have his blood on your hands."

"Enough. Go home, Patty. This is getting us nowhere."

Patty pointed the pistol at her heart. "You ruined my life and T.D.'s. You have to pay for that, Jinx."

"I TOLD YOU going to Wyoming was a bad idea," Brick said weakly as he gave Ella a lopsided smile.

Ella started on her cot next to his hospital bed. Tears instantly flooded her eyes as she shot to her feet to take his hand. "You had me so scared," she said, never so happy to see that grin of his.

"Angus?" he asked, his voice hoarse with emotion and no doubt pain as he looked around the hospital room. Of course he would know that Angus would be right here beside his bed, as well—if he could. "Ella?" There was a worried edge to her cousin's voice.

"He's going to be fine. He went after T.D., got hit in the head, but the doctor said other than a concussion and a few scrapes and bruises, he'll be fine. He's here in the hospital. You'll get to see him soon."

Brick seemed to relax. "I knew something had happened. I had this dream…" He seemed to shudder. He met her gaze. "I almost didn't make it, didn't I?" She nodded and swallowed the lump in her throat. "And T.D.?"

"He was wounded but got away."

"Jinx?"

"She was given medical attention and released. You'll hear all about it, once you've had some rest."

Brick closed his eyes. "I remember you and a helicopter?" he asked, opening his eyes again.

She nodded. "I was able to get cell phone service and called for help. You and I were flown to the hospital. Max rode with Jinx."

"Is Max okay?"

"He was admitted to the hospital for observation. The doctor doesn't think he had a heart attack but wanted to monitor him."

"T.D. got away?"

"Half the county is up on that mountain looking for him. They'll find him."

"I hope you're right." He reached for her hand and squeezed it. "When you see Angus…"

She nodded, tears burning her eyes. "I'll tell him that you miss him."

Brick smiled. "Tell him that I love him, okay? I'll deny I said it." He shrugged.

She had to smile, knowing he was telling the truth. "Your mother just went down the hall to get some coffee. Your dad flew down to Jackson Hole to see if he could help find T.D. since there was nothing he could do here but wait."

"That sounds like him. How's Mom?"

"Worried but you know Dana. She's as strong as they come. The rest of the family has been in and out. They're going to be delighted to hear that you're conscious and your old self."

Brick met her gaze. "I don't feel much like my old self right now. But it's so good to see you." He frowned. "Ella, what aren't you telling me?"

"You just worry about getting out of this bed and back on your feet."

"Ella?"

"It's my mother." She shook her head. "It's just this feeling. I'm sure it's nothing. Dana said she's minding the ranch while everyone else is down here."

She could see that he was drowsy and struggling to keep his eyes open. "You rest. Everything is fine now." And yet she couldn't shake the feeling that her mother was in some kind of trouble.

"TELL ME YOU found him," Angus said as the sheriff stepped into his room. He could see that the lawman looked exhausted.

"I'm afraid not," Harvey Bessler said as he removed his hat. "We'll resume the search in the morning."

Angus swore, making his already aching head hurt more. He'd been so hopeful when he'd been told how many were up on the mountain looking for T.D., his own father included. "You know Jinx won't be safe until T.D. is caught."

The sheriff nodded. "I just talked to Jinx before I came in to check on you. She's fine. I'm sending a deputy out there to keep an eye on her. Now, get some rest and quit worrying."

He watched the sheriff leave, wishing he could quit worrying. Common sense told him that T.D. was wounded and probably still up there on that mountain. Even if he'd gotten off it, he was in no shape to be going after Jinx again. The sheriff was right. He shouldn't worry.

But he did. Glancing around his hospital room, he spotted two things that helped him make up his mind about what to do about his worry. He saw his dirty clothing piled up on a chair by the bathroom door. He also saw his mother's coat and purse. Earlier, she'd been sitting next to his bed before going to check on Brick.

Angus quickly rose from the bed. He had to stop for a moment until the light-headedness passed. Struggling into his clothing, he questioned what good he would be to Jinx if his instincts were right and T.D. had somehow gotten off the mountain and headed for her ranch.

In his mother's purse, he found the keys for the rental car she'd told him about. He felt a little stronger. At least he told himself he did as he quietly opened the door and peered out.

It was so late that the hallway was empty. He headed for the exit sign, knowing he couldn't rest until he made sure Jinx was all right.

"PATTY, WHY WOULD you kill me?" Jinx demanded, seeing the gun waver in the woman's hand.

"Because someone has to do it!" she cried. "Otherwise, T.D. will never be free of you, and you know it."

Jinx thought of Wyatt Hanson in the trees, holding his rifle before riding away. Who had he been trying to shoot? Her or T.D.? "You think shooting me is going to free him for you? You'll be in prison." So would T.D., though she didn't mention that. "What happens when he comes off that mountain and finds out that you're in jail for shooting me?"

Tears filled Patty's eyes. "You really think he's alive?"

"Knowing T.D., I would count on it," she said truthfully.

The gun seemed to grow heavy in Patty's hand. "I don't want to live without him."

"You won't have to, unless you shoot me," Jinx told her. "Don't throw away your future." She could see that this had been a flawed plan of Patty's to start with. The woman wanted Jinx out of her life badly enough that she thought she could shoot her. Jinx understood that on some level. She wanted T.D. out of hers just as badly.

"Put the gun down, Patty." The male voice at the door made them both jump. Startled, Patty pulled the trigger, the pistol bucking in her hand. For the second time that day, Jinx felt a bullet buzz past her head. This one, though, didn't break the skin.

T.D. swore, his bellow almost drowned out by the report of the gun. He moved quickly for a man who was injured, grabbing the pistol and backhanding Patty, sending her flying to the floor at the corner of the room.

"I wasn't going to kill her!" Patty cried as T.D. turned the gun on her.

Without thinking, Jinx started to rush T.D. as if she thought she could stop him from killing the woman.

He swung the barrel of the pistol in her direction as he said, "I wouldn't if I were you." She froze where she was. She could tell that T.D. was weak from his gunshot wound even though he'd apparently gotten some sort of medical help. She could see part of the bandage sticking out of the collar of his shirt. But Jinx wasn't fool enough to think that would even the odds if she rushed him.

"Okay," he said, sounding as exhausted as she felt. "Now, tell me what the hell is going on here."

Patty was crying, still on the floor. "I just wanted to free you of her. I thought if she was dead…"

T.D. nodded, not taking his eyes off Jinx. "I stopped by your apartment before I came here," he said, without looking at Patty. Jinx heard the woman let out a cry as if he'd kicked her. "Had a little talk with Wyatt." Patty began to sob, her words lost in her tears. Jinx heard enough, though, to know that the woman had put Wyatt up to killing her up on that mountain. Now T.D. knew it, too.

"Did you really think that if you got Wyatt to kill Jinx that I would want anything to do with you?"

"We could get married," Patty said between sobs. "I would make you happy. You know I could."

"No, Patty, you and I are never getting married, especially after you almost got me killed. I will never love you the way I did Jinx. Never. You need to leave now, Patty. I don't think you want to watch what happens next."

Patty quit crying and wiped her face. "What are you going to do? You're in enough trouble. You can't kill her."

"Oh, I'm not going to kill her," he said, narrowing his eyes at Jinx. "Though she might wish I was when I'm through with her. Now, get out of here."

Patty got to her feet, hesitated and then rushed out the door.

T.D. hadn't moved. He seemed to be waiting until he heard a car engine to make sure Patty was gone before he said to Jinx, "Take off your clothes."

ANGUS DROVE UP the road to the Flying J Bar MC Ranch as fast as he dared. It had only been a few days since he and his brother and cousin had driven up this road. So much had changed in that time.

He pulled in behind the sheriff's department car and got out, telling himself this was probably a fool's errand. Just as the sheriff had said, there was a deputy watching the house.

But as he came along the side of the car, his heart began to pound. The deputy would have seen him drive up. He would have gotten out of his car to see who it was. That was if he could.

As Angus reached the driver's side, he saw the deputy slumped over in the seat and swore. His first instinct was to race into the house. But he was smart enough to know that in his physical state, he might need all the help he could get. He eased open the deputy's car door, grabbed the car radio and called it in. Once the dispatcher told him that help was on the way, he headed for the house.

JINX LOOKED ACROSS the expanse of her bed at T.D. "You know I'm not taking off my clothes."

He chuckled. "It was worth a try." He put the pistol down on the nightstand. As he did, she bolted for the door. Of course he beat her to it, knowing exactly what she would do. Grabbing a handful of her hair, he dragged her back into the room and threw her on the bed.

She could tell the effort hurt him, just as she knew it wouldn't stop him. He knew this was the very last thing she wanted from him so he was more determined than ever. He climbed on top of her, and holding her down, began to rip off her clothing as he told her—as he had on the mountain—all the things he was going to do to her. Only this time, there was no one to stop him.

Even with him injured, she was no match for him. She knew she should just submit, just as she knew she wasn't about to.

The sound of the gunshot startled her. She looked up into T.D.'s sneering face as she felt his hold on her lessen. The second shot made him jerk. The third crumpled him on top of her.

Jinx felt his warm blood spreading over her chest. She pushed him off and leaped up from the bed to see the shooter standing in the shadowed doorway of her bedroom.

"Patty?" she whispered, seeing the glazed-over look in the woman's eyes and the gun still clutched in her hand, the barrel now pointed at Jinx.

"The two of you didn't even notice me come back into the room," the woman said. "The two of you were so busy that you didn't even see me pick up the gun."

"You know I wanted none of that," Jinx said, and saw something in the woman's expression that turned her blood to ice. "Don't make this worse, Patty."

"How could it be worse?" she asked on a sob. "I loved him. I would have done anything for him.

Anything. But all he wanted was…you." She raised the gun to heart level and pressed the trigger.

ANGUS HAD BEEN moving stealthily down the hall toward the sound of voices when he'd heard the first gunshot. By the second gunshot, he was running. By the third, he'd reached the woman standing in the doorway of the bedroom.

Before she could pull the trigger again, he slammed into her. The report was like an explosion to his already pounding head. The woman went down. He went down with her as he fought to get the pistol out of her hand.

"Let me kill her!" the woman was screaming. "Please… You don't know what she's done. She ruined my life." She'd broken into sobs but was still fighting for the gun as they wrestled on the floor.

Normally, Angus could have easily disarmed the woman, but his head injury had left him weak and slow as if he was moving through quicksand.

Out of the corner of his eye, he saw Jinx and was instantly thankful she didn't appear to have been shot. She stepped down on the woman's hand holding the gun, grinding her boot heel in until he heard a cry and Jinx kicked the gun away.

He sat back against the wall, the gun at his side, as Jinx dropped to the floor next to him.

"What are you doing here?" she demanded. "You should be in the hospital."

Angus could only smile because he had to agree. "I was worried about you."

"Oh, Angus." She cupped his face and bent to kiss him. The sound of sirens filled the air, drowning out at least some of Patty's sobs. The woman had climbed up on the bed and now had T.D.'s head cradled in her lap. She was smoothing back his hair and telling him about a dream she had that involved Disney World.

Chapter Twenty-Two

"What's the plan now?" Marshal Hudson Savage asked from the head of the huge family table in the dining room at Cardwell Ranch.

"Don't cross examine them, sweetheart," Dana said sweetly but strongly. "They've been through enough without having to decide their futures at my dinner table right this moment. Have some more roast beef," she said to her twin sons seated across from her.

"I'm going back to Wyoming to help Jinx get everything ready for the sale of her ranch," Angus said, passing on more roast beef.

Brick took some, though, thanking their mother. "Mom, everything is delicious," he said after chewing and swallowing. His recovery was going slowly, making them all worried about him.

She smiled. "Thank you, Brick. You know you both gave us a scare. I'm just so glad that you're home."

"But for how long this time?" Hud asked, not

to be deterred. Brick hadn't looked up from his meal, eating quietly as if lost in his own thoughts.

"I shouldn't be gone for more than a couple of weeks," Angus said. "Then my plan is to come back and go to work here on the ranch." He said this to his mother. "That's if you'll have me."

His mother's eyes filled with tears. "Really?"

"Finally," Hud grumbled. "You boys are going to be the death of me."

"Are you coming back…alone?" she asked, pretending interest in the small portion of mashed potatoes on her plate.

Angus laughed. "You are so subtle, Mom."

"Like a sledgehammer," his father muttered under his breath.

"Well?" she asked, clearly ignoring her husband.

"Alone, Mom. At least for now. Jinx and I both need some time."

"What about you?" Hud asked Brick.

"I've actually been thinking about what I might want to do once I'm healed," he said, motioning to the sling that had his mother cutting his meat up as if he was five. Angus could tell that his brother didn't mind. Like him, Brick seemed to be glad to be home. "I heard you might have an opening for a deputy marshal."

His father looked up from his meal in surprise. "Are you serious about this?"

Brick nodded. "I am."

"You have to go to the law academy, but if this is something you want…"

Angus could tell that their father was delighted at the prospect that at least one of their sons might be interested in law enforcement. Their older brother Hank lived on the ranch with his wife, Frankie, and Mary did the ranch's books. It had looked like they all might be involved in ranch work in this family.

He looked over at their mother. Clearly she'd prefer Brick not become a lawman, but she only took her husband's hand and smiled at Brick. "It will be nice to have you boys home," Hud said.

"I'll get dessert," Dana said and got up to hurry into the kitchen. Angus could tell that she was thinking about all the meals the family would be having at this table in the future. Tonight she'd wanted it to be just the four of them. But he knew they were in for a lot of big family celebrations at this table.

When his mother returned with a three-tiered chocolate cake, he said, "By the way, I thought Ella was going to be here tonight."

Dana shook her head as she began to cut the cake. Brick already had his fork ready and was saying how much he'd missed his mother's cooking, making her beam.

"Ella?" she said. "She wasn't around. Hank told me that he saw her leave." She stopped cutting to look up at him. "I think she's gone to look for her mother."

"Stacy?" Brick said as he took the slice of cake his mother handed him. "Where's she off to?" he asked and took a large bite of the cake and thick fudge-like frosting, one of his mother's favorite recipes.

"That's just it," Dana said. "We don't know. Stacy just left." She looked to her husband, who shook his head. "Maybe she just needs a break from all of us."

"Maybe," Angus said, but he could tell that his mother was worried about her sister.

"Ella will find her," Brick said. "That woman is like a bloodhound when she gets something in her head."

"I hope you're right," their mother said as she handed Angus his cake. "Now, tell me about Jinx. I want to know everything."

ON A BEAUTIFUL fall day, JoRay "Jinx" McCallahan drove into Cardwell Ranch in her pickup, pulling a horse trailer with her favorite horse inside. She slowed as she crossed the bridge over the Gallatin River to look down. The water was incredibly clear, a pale green that made the granite rocks along the bottom shine as if pure gold.

She breathed in the fall air scented with the river and the pines and looked up at the towering mountain with its rock cliffs before letting herself take in the ranch. The house was two stories with a red metal roof. And there was the large old barn that she recalled as a young girl.

Jinx smiled, thinking how strange life was that she was here again. Only this time, she couldn't wait to see that cowboy she'd pushed out that barn window all those years ago. Time heals all wounds, her father used to say. To some extent that was true. She still missed her father just as she missed the Flying J Bar MC Ranch she'd grown up on.

But it was a dull ache overpowered by the excitement she felt to be on the Cardwell Ranch again. She actually had butterflies flitting around in her stomach at just the thought of seeing Angus after these months apart. They'd talked on the phone for hours every day about everything but the future. Angus had left the door open.

"I'll be here if you ever want to come north again," he'd said. "I'll be waiting."

Angus was in the barn when he saw the truck and horse trailer coming up the road. He stepped out, pulling his Stetson down to shade his eyes. He couldn't see who was behind the wheel. His heart leaped anyway. He'd been waiting for this day for too long not to know it had finally come.

As Jinx pulled up into the yard, he strode toward her truck, trying hard not to run. She opened the door and stepped out. Her beautiful copper hair caught the autumn sun. She reached back into the pickup for her straw hat and putting it on, looked in his direction.

By then, he was closing the distance between them, running toward their future. When he reached her, he grabbed her, wrapping his arms around her and lifting her into the air. She laughed, a sound that filled his heart with joy. Slowly, he lowered her back to the ground and looked into her beautiful freckled face. Now he would have all the time in the world to count every one of them, he thought and glanced into the warm honey of her eyes.

"Jinx," he said on a breath as light as a caress.

"Angus." She smiled, those eyes glinting. "You said to just drive up when I felt like it. I felt like it."

He laughed as his heart swelled to overflowing. "I'm so glad. Wait until you taste my biscuits."

She laughed. "You still have that bet going with Max?"

He nodded. "He promised to come up to the ranch." Angus looked into her eyes and knew that if he'd had a preacher standing by, he'd have married this woman right here and now. Looping his arm around her waist he pulled her to him and kissed her as if there was no tomorrow.

At the sound of the front door of the house banging open, he let her go. "Two seconds from now we are going to be mobbed by my family. Before that happens, I need to tell you something. I love you."

She nodded. "I love you, Angus."

"That's good because I don't have to look over my shoulder to know that the woman hurrying this way is my mother. She's going to want to know when we're getting married. I don't want to rush you but…"

Jinx looked over his shoulder, then back at him, grinning. "If that's a proposal—"

He dropped to one knee, pulled out the small velvet box he'd been carrying around for months. "It certainly is. Say yes. Please. The engagement can be as long as you want, I promise."

She laughed and nodded. "Yes."

He opened the box, took out the ring and slipped it on her finger. He heard his mother's cry of glee behind him.

"It's beautiful, Angus," Jinx said and kissed him as he rose to his feet again. "I don't need a long engagement since I've known for a long time I want to spend the rest of my life with you."

"Oh," Dana cried. "That is so beautiful." Then she was hugging the two of them as more family members began to show up.

Angus introduced his large family and extended family until the yard was full of Cardwells and Savages. It was as if they'd known today was the day to be on the ranch. He wondered if his mother had anything to do with this.

"I should have warned you about my family," Angus whispered to Jinx. "You can still change your mind."

Jinx shook her head. "Not a chance, cowboy."

"I'd like to tell you that it won't always be like this," he said.

"I love it." She looked around at all of them, most talking over the others as if her arriving had turned into a party. "I remember you telling me about your mother wanting all of your boots around her big dining room table. I want my boots under that table."

"You're killing me, Jinx," he said as he pulled her to him again for a kiss. "I can't tell you how long I've wanted this with you."

She nodded, her eyes bright with tears. "It's strange but I feel as if I've always been headed back here. I know it sounds crazy, especially knowing how hard it was for me to sell my family's ranch, but driving in just now, I had the strangest feeling that I've come home."

Angus pulled her closer. "Welcome home. Trust me, now that you're going to be a part of Cardwell Ranch, you should know it's going to be a wild ride."

* * * * *

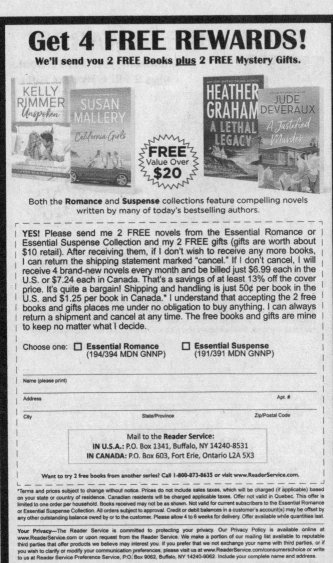

#1935 DOUBLE ACTION DEPUTY
Cardwell Ranch: Montana Legacy • by B.J. Daniels
When Montana deputy marshal Brick Savage asks homicide detective
Maureen Mortensen to help him find the person who destroyed her family, she
quickly accepts his offer. But as the stakes rise and they get closer than they ever
expected, can they find the killer before they become targets?

#1936 RUNNING OUT OF TIME
Tactical Crime Division • by Cindi Myers
To find out who poisoned some medications, two TCD agents go undercover and
infiltrate the company posing as a married couple. But as soon as Jace Cantrell
and Laura Smith arrive at Stroud Pharmaceuticals, someone ups the ante by
planting explosives in their midst.

#1937 CHAIN OF CUSTODY
Holding the Line • by Carol Ericson
When a baby lands on border patrol agent Nash Dillon's doorstep, Emily Lang,
an undercover investigator posing as a nanny, comes to his rescue. But once he
discovers why Emily is really there—and that both her and the baby's life are in
danger—he'll unleash every skill in his arsenal to keep them out of harm's way.

#1938 BADLANDS BEWARE
A Badlands Cops Novel • by Nicole Helm
When Detective Tucker Wyatt is sent to protect Rachel Knight from her father's
enemies, neither of them realizes exactly how much danger she's in. As she starts
making connections between her father's past and a current disappearance,
she's suddenly under attack from all sides.

#1939 A DESPERATE SEARCH
An Echo Lake Novel • by Amanda Stevens
Detective Adam Thayer is devastated when he fails to save his friend. But a series
of clues brings Adam to coroner Nikki Dresden, who's eager to determine if one
of the town's most beloved citizens was murdered. They must work together to
unravel a deadly web of lies and greed...or die trying.

#1940 WITNESS ON THE RUN
by Cassie Miles
WITSEC's Alyssa Bailey is nearly attacked until investigator Rafe Fournier comes
to her defense. Even so, Alyssa is unsure of who she can trust thanks to gaps in
her memory. Racing to escape whoever has discovered her whereabouts, they
soon learn what truths hide in the past.

HICNM0620

ReaderService.com has a new look!

We have refreshed our website and
we want to share our new look with you.
Head over to ReaderService.com
and check it out!

On ReaderService.com, you can:

- Try 2 free books from any series
- Access risk-free special offers
- View your account history & manage payments
- Browse the latest Bonus Bucks catalog

Don't miss out!

If you want to stay up-to-date on the latest at the Reader Service and enjoy more Harlequin content, make sure you've signed up for our monthly News & Notes email newsletter. Sign up online at ReaderService.com.

RS19